STETSON

DANIELLE NORMAN

STETSON

By: Danielle Norman

So one night at band camp— just kidding.
But truthfully, Tina, bitch, head bitch, you are the shit.
Everything that you do to keep me straight (well sort of straight)
is impressive. I'll never be able to thank you enough.

Names are a curious thing and for that I would like to dedicate
this to all the people with nicknames especially those who have
no idea they've been nicknamed. After all it makes it so much
funnier when you have no idea.
Kind of like the President of our HOA- Seymour Asshole
The woman who sits next to me when I get my hair done
practicing her Kegels- Ophelia Dix.
And finally the guys who send random shit to me on facebook like
it is a fucking dating site- Sawyer Skank

Saddle up and don't look back.
You're not headed that way.

1

LONDON

Why were funeral home's chairs so uncomfortable? Did they have a catalog of nothing but hardwood, straight-back chairs? Chairs that constantly reminded you that you were uncomfortable, the people around you were uncomfortable, and that you were going to be uncomfortable for another two hours.

Maybe they did it so that you wouldn't be distracted from the people walking by and reminding you of how fabulous your father was or how every day since you learned about his lung cancer that you worried. Nope, they wouldn't want you to miss a second of being reminded of how worried you were about not being able to fill his shoes.

Worried that you would let your sisters down.

Worried that despite everything—despite your father having raised you to believe that girls were just as great as boys—maybe the farm might have been better off in the hands of a son. That was if Samuel Kelly had had a son, but he didn't. He'd been stuck with three daughters and a wife that had run off when the girls were little.

"I'm sorry for your loss." I was pulled from my thoughts and self-doubt to accept more condolences.

"Your family is in our prayers."

"Let us know if you girls need anything."

"Your father was a good man."

Were condolences like straws and everyone drew one; whatever was written on the straw was the platitude you had to repeat?

I looked at my sisters to make sure that they were holding up. Part of me felt relieved because I knew that Daddy wasn't in pain anymore, but at the same time, I was pissed at him for leaving us. It didn't matter that I was thirty —nothing made you feel like you were a little girl all over again than losing a parent.

The pastor finished the service, and my sisters and I followed the pallbearers, who carried my father's casket out the doors of the church.

Sweat trickled down my back, and I found myself more focused on the riding lawn mower I could see in the distance than I was on what was being said as they lowered Daddy's casket into the ground. Taking a deep breath, I inhaled the scent of fresh mowed grass and impending rain. It was going to rain, I could smell the saltiness in the air, and when I opened my mouth I could taste the saltiness on the tip of my tongue.

Who was I kidding? It always rained in Florida, especially this time of the year, and the rain was always salty thanks to being close to the ocean. But right then I needed the rain, I begged for it. I wanted it to pour and send all these people scurrying for cover so that I could sit here for a few moments and say goodbye to my hero.

I was on autopilot, my focus was up toward the horizon and the rain rolling in, while people were kissing my cheek, saying goodbye, and then walking off. Person after person stopped, but I was moving out of natural reaction.

"You okay, London?" I looked at my sister Paris as she tucked a few loose strands of hair behind my ear. "You seem like you're a million miles away."

"I'm fine, just tired. Let's go home." I stood and held out one hand for each of my sisters. Being the oldest, I'd always felt a heavy amount of responsibility for them, and right then, I needed not to be the weak one.

The three of us headed to my truck. Jumping up into the seat, I paused for a second before pulling my legs in to kick off any excess dirt that still clung to my heels. Nothing about Geneva was fancy, not even the cemetery, where I had to walk through, dirt, sand, and stand in soft sod while I watched my father be lowered into the ground. After removing my hat—because in our little town you always wore a black hat to a funeral—I laid it on the console and started the engine. As I glanced into my rearview mirror, I met the eyes of my baby sister Holland, who hadn't said a word, which was so strange since of the three of us, she was always the most outspoken one.

But I wanted to get this day over with, which was probably why we had bucked tradition and decided not to have a potluck after the funeral. People from the church had been bringing food by for the last month while Daddy was in hospice. I just didn't want any more people traipsing in and out of the house telling us how sorry they were, which in the end ultimately led them to discussing the fact that none of us were married and someone was bound to offer up one of their relatives to help us out. As if we were so desperate to find a husband that we needed someone to give us their cousin's son, who was probably still living in his mom's basement and went by the name of Bubba. No thanks.

I drove the five miles to our home, the one that I grew up in, the one that still smelled of oiled leather. The smell was an ever-present reminder of when Dad would bring the saddles in and sit there with a polishing cloth, and I realized that I wasn't ready to go in, not yet.

"You coming?" Holland stood in the doorway, front door ajar, waiting for me.

"Hey, I'll be back later. I'm going up to Marcus's."

Or, more specifically, the Elbow Room, which was the bar he owned. Holland nodded, and I was back in my truck before the door even closed behind her.

Fifteen minutes later, I was pulling open the door and walking into the dimly lit space that smelled of old smoke. It had been a few years since people were allowed to smoke inside, but the scent that was imbedded into the structure assuaged me. That smell wasn't ever leaving. I remember when the previous owner had the place and my daddy would bring me up here as a kid, there were nights that the smoke had been so thick you could practically cut it with a knife. There had been no hope for the air filtration system to keep up.

I waved at Marcus, who had already changed out of his dark suit and was wearing a T-shirt with the bar's logo on the back, and slid into an empty stool. He and his brother had been two of Daddy's pallbearers, but you wouldn't have known it if you hadn't been there. He looked as if today was just another day.

"Well, I do believe I have my passport ready," he hollered. I knew that he was trying to lift my spirits.

"You may see London and you may see France, but you'll

never see my underpants." I retorted, and I caught the beer he slid me down the well-worn pine top bar.

I was used to all the comments and jokes about my name, had to be. When you were raised with two sisters and you all had names of fancy destinations, people expected you to be well...fancy. They were always shocked to realize that the only thing fancy about the Kelly girls were their names. The fancy one had been our mama, which was why she ran off with the first guy who promised to show her the world when I was ten years old. She'd wanted more than farm life. But not me, I could spend my days running the fields on Madam Mim, my horse.

I downed my first beer, slammed the bottle onto the counter a bit too hard, and smiled when I realized that Marcus had been anticipating my mood and had the second one waiting. I started drinking as I scanned the room. The place was a cross between a dive bar and a honky-tonk. The walls were crowded with memorabilia from locals who had made it big or famous people who had visited. There were several photos from the movie *The Waterboy* with Adam Sandler since the bonfire party was actually filmed right here in Geneva, Florida. They also filmed a few episodes of *ER* with George Clooney here. That was when I was young and boys were still yucky, but I remembered all the moms and teachers going crazy.

M.J. Tucker, a guy I went to high school with, was sitting at one of the corner booths, and I shook my head. I seriously considered calling his wife since he was hitting on Etta Hill. She knew—hell, everyone knew that M.J. was married. Then again, we also knew that Etta's last name suited her perfectly, she was still the easiest hill to climb. Some things never changed, no matter how long it had been since high school.

"Another one, please." I turned to face Marcus to make sure that he'd heard me. He was standing behind the counter, lost in space.

I took a long swig, I hadn't realized how thirsty I'd been, two beers in ten minutes was fast even for me. Shaking my head at my realization, I followed the direction of Marcus's gaze and saw a couple of women wearing denim miniskirts and crop tops. I fought back my urge to laugh at their shiny new cowboy boots. They were wannabes. Wannabe cowgirls, wannabe older than they were, and wannabe someone's one-night stand.

Rolling my eyes, I waved a hand in front of Marcus's face to get his attention. The man always lost his shit around booty and breasts. Once again, some things never changed.

I cleared my throat and waited with a giant grin on my face.

"Holy shit, London, you just got here. You might want to slow down a bit." He cleared away the bottle but still reached behind him and grabbed me another.

"Don't judge, you know damn well that it's been a hard day."

"But you're driving." Marcus tried to argue before handing me the bottle. "Just promise me that you aren't leaving until I say so."

I chuckled dryly and nodded. Yeah, I had no intention of wrapping myself around some telephone pole.

"How you holding up?"

"Really? I'm in a bar, dressed all in black, and resembling a lost little girl. Worse yet, I feel like one. Can we talk about something else, anything?" I took a swig from the bottle and wiped my mouth with the back of my hand. Not the most ladylike action, but it was fitting for the way I was feeling.

"Have you checked out the latest *Hustler* magazine?"

"Holy shit, Marcus." I laughed so hard I almost choked on my drink. "Don't tell me you read that shit. Oh my god, I don't know that I've ever seen one."

"That's my girl, that's the laugh I've been missing." Marcus reached forward and wrapped his giant paw of a hand around mine.

"You know you wouldn't have to resort to those types of magazines if you'd stop being such a commitment-phobe. I swear that I don't know who is more sex depraved, you or the women you hook up with."

I'd been ragging on him since high school when our world was divided into two groups: helmet head or fans of helmet heads. And group two was what the helmet heads called Future Fags of America, otherwise known as FFA. Marcus and I were FFA all because we grew up on farms. But both groups had their own set of popular kids, except for Marcus, he was the one that was determined to buck the system. He wanted to sample the goods on both sides of the fence.

"Look who's talking. When was your last relationship? Oh wait, never because you are too damn committed to the ranch. You need to get out and have some fun, let loose. We need to go out sometime—you can be my wingman and help me find someone and I'll help you."

"God, I love you, Marcus, but the last thing I want to do is let you loose on my own species. You are what I like to call a man whore."

Trying to feign injury, he threw his hands over his heart and acted as if my words were causing him to have a heart attack.

"You know that does not work on me, right?"

"If you disapprove of my love life so much, then maybe

you should be my dating coach, tell me what I'm doing wrong and how to find, you know, the one."

Whoosh, my beer spewed everywhere. "Fuck, warn a girl next time you're going to say something like that, won't you?"

"Is someone choking? I know mouth-to-mouth. Hey, Marcus, a bottle of beer, please."

I turned at the familiar baritone voice and tried to ignore the way it sent shivers straight to all the right parts of me. I slowly moved my eyes from his boots up his jeans, to his black T-shirt, and then to the gorgeous face. Yep, speaking of man whore, it was Braden Fucking McManus.

"You okay there, London? I'm assuming that you really don't need mouth-to-mouth."

"That's debatable, depends who's asking. If you're offering." I threw my hands over my mouth. Oh shit, I said that aloud. It was supposed to stay in my head. Beer, I had beer tongue. That slippery thing that held nothing in.

Braden coughed, making me think that maybe he was the one that needed the mouth-to-mouth and I'd be willing to practice on him.

Embracing my alcohol-infused bravado, I dropped my hand and gave him a wink instead of cowering away from my slip-up.

"You'll have to excuse her, Deputy, she's had a bit much tonight." Marcus laughed as he looked at me and tried to extract the bottle from my hands, but I held on for dear life.

"Shut up, this is only my third," I mumbled to Marcus even though he wasn't paying attention. Oh my God, this was Braden fucking McManus. I'd had a crush on him since we were in middle school. Of course, we never spoke because he was too busy being homecoming king, prom king, and the class president. He'd always been so out of my league.

I averted my gaze from Marcus and turned toward Braden. His muscled arms flexing was almost as good as watching porn. I could totally get off to this. Damn. The protruding veins made it difficult not to look at him.

Braden moved his arm to take a swig off his bottle, and it finally broke my hypnotic lock on him. I glanced up and noticed that he'd been watching me.

I gave him a head bob.

What?

I gave him a fucking head bob. The only thing missing was the Jersey accent, and I would have been all Joey Tribbiani from friends. "How you doin'?" I wasn't cool. I couldn't pull that off. What was I saying? Even Joey Tribbiani couldn't pull that off.

"So, Sergeant, what are you doing in here tonight?" Marcus continued talking as if I hadn't just made a fool of myself. I owed the guy a home cooked meal. Thank you, Marcus.

"I'm a lieutenant now. But Braden is fine. I just got assigned back to the East District, so I thought I'd pop in."

The two chatted about Braden being back in Geneva, and I sat there listening. God, even his neck was sexy.

Braden cut his attention to me. "How you doing, London? I heard about your dad. I'm sorry for your loss."

I nodded my thanks and took another swig of my beer.

"Is it true that you're going to stay and run the ranch?"

"Mm-hmm." Voice, London, use your voice, I mentally reprimanded myself. "Yeah, my sisters and I. We each have our own skills anyway. I've always handled the books and the cattle ranch, Holland is a horse whisperer if there ever was one, and Paris is a whiz with organic stuff. She keeps our fields beautiful so the horses and cattle always have new grazing areas. Between the three of us, we might equal one Samuel Kelly."

"I'm sure you'll make your dad proud."

Marcus smirked playfully as he stole glances at me, trying to tear me from my melancholy and tease me because he knew that I'd had a crush on Braden McManus since we were in sixth grade. I swallowed the lump that formed in my throat and shot Marcus a deadly glare. Braden looked at me, then nodded lightly. He had this presence about him, and it was overwhelming.

Or at least I was overwhelmed when he slid onto the barstool next to me and made himself comfortable as if he was going to stay a while. The air around me got thin, making it hard to breathe.

I studied his face a bit longer in the dim lighting of the club. He was absolutely one of those men who only got better looking with age. He was rugged with his steel jaw, which seemed to have been carved by an expert sculptor and gave him a calculated edginess. His hair was almost black and was messy in a way that could have been an accident or could have taken him fifteen minutes to get it to look like that. His mouth...oh, that mouth, it was curled into a friendly, inviting grin.

I'd bend over backward for my sisters, but Braden McManus, I'd bend over forward for.

Damn it, London, don't go there.

The trance I was in was broken when I heard Marcus faking a cough. Out of the corner of my eyes, I saw his mouth crack in to a mischievous grin. "So, Braden, how's the family?" Marcus asked as he grabbed a cloth and wiped off the bar.

"Good, Mom and Dad still live in the same house. I think

that my mom is enjoying being retired, but my dad is bored as hell."

"How about your wife?" Marcus held up one finger. "Hold that thought." Marcus turned to answer the phone, which left me with nothing to do but wonder who the hell Braden had married. Was he happy? I bet she was beautiful. He probably married some cheerleader type.

"Hey, I gotta run, that was my mom." Marcus lifted the half-door that kept people from walking behind the bar.

"Is everything okay?" I leaned forward on my elbows, and my heart ached with worry for Marcus and his brother, Asher. Marcus's mom was several years older than my dad had been, and something happening to her today of all days was almost too much.

"Yeah, she's fine, but I have to run. Don't worry about your tab; they're on me. If you need anything else, just ask Jett." He gestured toward the bartender at the other end of the bar before adding, "Braden, it was nice seeing you, and I hope you stop in again."

"I'll start coming by more." Braden held out his hand, and the men shook before Marcus turned to me. "Listen to me, call your sisters or call my brother, hear me?"

"Don't worry about it, I'll make sure she's fine," Braden assured him.

I rolled my eyes and then gave Marcus my most motherly stare. "I better not find out that you skipped out for some booty call. You know that it's okay to have a dick with standards."

I turned my gaze to Braden, who was beating his chest and making a loud choking noise. "You okay there?" I patted his back and felt his body heat radiate through my fingers.

"Yep, I might be the one who needs mouth-to-mouth. I just never imagined hearing London Kelly saying something like that. The girl I remember was much quieter."

Marcus let out a loud snort. "Amazing how girls can fool you, huh?"

I shook my head, trying to clear away the thoughts of putting my mouth to Braden's mouth, and decided that one more beer shouldn't hurt, four wasn't going to kill me, it would just help get rid of that thing...shit...what was it called? Oh yeah, a filter. "Jett, can you hand me another beer?"

2

BRADEN

My cheeks hurt. Ever since walking into the Elbow Room, I hadn't stopped smiling. London was hysterical, and I'd never imagined she had this side. Back in high school, she always seemed shy, or at least every time I came near her she was.

"What are you staring at, Braden McManus?"

"You do know that you can just call me Braden, right? You don't have to use my last name."

She tilted her head slightly as if pondering my words. Clearly, London was nervous, and I had no idea why.

"Nope. I'll stick to Braden McManus, thank you very much."

"But we've known each other since we were, what, ten?"

"Eleven."

"So, you know that we were eleven when we met, but you won't call me by just my first name?"

"Nope. Bad things happen when girls start getting all cozy with guys like you." She stuck out her index finger and poked me in the chest then moved her hand to smooth out the wrinkle she'd just put in my shirt.

"What's wrong with guys like me?" I was provoking her —I knew I was. But she was so cute and she was still patting me.

"You're too good looking, and that makes you a danger to womankind."

"Am I danger to you, London?" I leaned close and inhaled the combination of hay, flowers, and maple syrup that made her smell like Southern sunshine. I wasn't sure why, but at that moment, those had to be the most erotic scents in the world.

"Nope, not a danger. See, I'm smart and won't get buddy-buddy with you. I grew up around ranch hands. I don't like guys like you, ones that only want to get into my pants, so I'm rejecting you before anything can even start."

Her hand had stopped patting and was resting on my pec. I doubted she realized she was even doing it. "Okay, London, so how many drinks have you had?"

"Believe it or not this is only my fourth. I've had a hard day. Hell, I've had a hard last few weeks. I feel like I'm drowning. I came in for an escape." She folded her arms on top of the bar and rested her head on them as she used her waist to make the bar stool swivel.

Geneva was a tiny town, we had one stoplight, one school, and one store that doubled as the gas station and meeting place. Word spread pretty fast when Samuel Kelly died, and as much as I wanted to pay my respects, it felt weird. I didn't know the man. I'd only known London because we went to the same school.

When we were younger, she'd always smile and wave, but once we got to high school, I barely even get a nod. It was as if we became strangers. It was weird how something from back then could seem like it was yesterday.

"Sooo, Braden McManus, you never answered the

question, are you married? Where's the wife? Whatever happened to that cheerleader?"

"No, London Kelly, I'm not married, which means that I don't have a wife, and what cheerleader?"

"You know the one." London swung one arm out at me, and I had to place a hand on the back of the barstool to keep it steady and her in it.

"Nope, I have no clue what you're talking about."

"Ugh. Lie. All men lie, and you Braden McManus are the worst. Missy, or was it Krissy? Shit. Maybe her name was Sissy? I don't know, but you and she were always sucking face. I'd walk down the halls and there you two were, going at it. In the parking lot, in the library—hell, even in the gym. I figured that you two would have gotten married and had a shitload of kids by now the way she was always dry humping you in public."

"London, you have me pegged all wrong."

"Whatever. It isn't like I care anyway. You know what? Forget I said anything. I mean look at me, I'm thirty years old, single, and except for Marcus, I can't tell you the last time a guy paid me a compliment."

"You haven't changed one bit, you are still just as beautiful as you were back then and just as feisty."

"What are you doing?"

"I'm complimenting you." I winked at her, knowing that she'd take my compliment as a joke.

"Haha, very funny. Just remember that today when I woke up and spun the wheel of attitude, it landed on sarcastic bitch, again. So, no need to lie to me."

Jett slid a basket of cheesesticks and some sliders over to us and then gave me a pointed look between glancing to London. She, of course, didn't notice, but I nodded, happy that this beautiful girl had some solid people looking out for her.

"London, you do realize that not all people pay their compliments verbally, right? Some do it with actions."

She turned and stared at me, and our eyes locked. "Explain." She picked up a cheese stick and waited for me to talk.

"I was just thinking about Marcus and how he didn't want to leave until he knew that you were going to be okay and get home safe."

"Marcus is like a brother to me."

"But he isn't your brother. That's a compliment, out of everyone he knows, he actually chose you to be part of his family. And Jett keeps looking over here to make sure that you are okay. He brought food over just so you wouldn't keep drinking on an empty stomach. It's a compliment when someone chooses to care about you when they don't have to."

She grabbed a slider, took a bite, and chewed slowly as if pondering over what I had just said. She reached for the glass of water that Jett had brought when he set the food down, and I was hoping this meant she was over her pity party for the evening, not that she didn't deserve one. She absolutely did.

I reached across her and pulled the basket of cheese sticks closer but stopped when she trailed one finger down my cheek. Looking to my left, I watched her eyes, but they weren't looking at me, well, they were, they were just focused on my lips. Her mouth was lightly parted, and she was slowly leaning in to me. When her hands slipped around my neck and pulled me closer, I didn't resist. Her lips locked with mine in a way that was too graceful for someone who was drunk.

My shock only lasted a second, and then I was kissing her back, nipping her bottom lip before deepening the kiss and sliding my tongue against hers.

She pulled back and looked up at me, batting her lashes as she smiled impishly.

"I'm ready to go home." She rose from her seat and leaned sideways dangerously.

"Whoa, let me help you." I wrapped an arm around her waist to steady her. Supporting her weight wasn't that hard because she was light as feather. The warmth of her body sent tingles down my spine. She was so fucking soft.

"Are you okay?" She held her eyes shut and then leaned her head against my shoulder.

"London?" I whispered, slightly shaking her shoulders, but she just groaned in response.

"Yeah, just stood up too fast. I'm not drunk, but I definitely can't drive home. I need to call one of my sisters." London reached for her purse.

Placing a hand on hers to still her search. "I got you, I'll take you home."

"You sure? I live way off 46."

"I know where the Kelly Ranch is." Releasing a deep breath, I shook my head at the sudden twist of events. I knew that I was only driving her home, but it gave me another chance, some more time to ask her out.

When we stepped outside into the muggy evening air, I placed one hand on London's back and escorted her toward my truck. She watched me with a slightly annoyed twist of her lips as I opened her door for her, and I wanted to laugh. The girl would need to start seeing the compliments in actions.

"Look, I'm appreciative of the ride home but that doesn't mean I'm incapable of doing normal shit, got it?"

London held her keys wrapped in both hands against her chest.

"Never thought you were incapable of doing anything you set your mind to. I was only trying to be nice. You've had a long day, you're in heels, and this is a gravel parking lot."

"Oh." London nodded, and I waited for her to get in and then ran around to start the engine and turn on the air conditioner for her.

"I think that I just need to get home," London said, her voice drowned out by the radio. I tilted my head to see her. She looked very peaceful and very innocent.

"No worries, I'm taking you home."

Driving down State Road 46, I followed the signs to Kelly Farms and Iron Horse Stables. This part of Seminole County was sparse, and everyone had acreage, so the traffic was non-existent. It wasn't uncommon to see people riding a horse down the side of the busy State Road either. Hell, I remember my dad used to make jokes because the grade school had a sign that read: No horses allowed on the sidewalk. He always used to laugh, wondering which idiot took their horse up on the school sidewalk because for there to be a sign, there had to be a reason.

It had been almost twelve years since I had been on this side of town, and the last time was when I was in high school and had gone to a party at Marcus's house.

"Is Marcus still your neighbor?"

"He is. The O'Neals sold their property about a week ago, though." She pointed to a large sold sign. "It's a shame we couldn't get it, but five hundred acres is a bit out of our price range."

"Have you met the new owners?"

"Nope. I'm sure I will eventually. The old owners said the guy was nice, but we will see."

When I pulled into the fenced area of the ranch, the house was all lit up outside but not inside. The home was beautiful, I didn't think I'd ever seen it before, but it was sprawling, the outside was covered in either cedar or cypress shake.

Pulling in front of the circle drive, I stole a glimpse of London, who was staring out the window as if deep in thought.

"London?"

"Mm-hmmm," she hummed distractedly.

I was sure that she didn't intend for her words to be erotic, but they were, and I felt like a total ass as I adjusted the front of my pants.

"Sweetheart, we're at your house."

London sat up and then turned to me. "Thank you for everything, not just bringing me home but listening to me. I'm total a mess, and I know it."

"You are a beautiful mess." I slid one hand to cup the side of her face. I wanted to kiss her again, to taste her before I let her go for the night.

She pulled one corner of her bottom lip in-between her teeth and looked at me between her lashes. Fuck, that had to be the most provocative pose in the world.

"Don't, London."

"Don't what?" She still watched me through her nearly closed eyes.

"Don't look at me that way. You're so fucking beautiful, and all I want to do is show you just how beautiful you are."

Her lashes slowly rose, and our eyes were locked as she unbuckled her seatbelt and shifted so she was sitting on her knees. Then she stretched over the center console and kissed me. I met her kiss touch for touch. I couldn't hold back, nor did I want to as I pulled her closer to me, urging her to crawl over the center console so she was straddling me. Adjusting the steering column and pushing my seat back, I made room for her, and neither of us dared to break the kiss.

When her fingers made their way to my shirt and the first breeze of cool air hit my chest, I knew that it was decision time. Either I stopped this or I was going to fuck this woman of one too many of my teenage fantasies right here.

My answer was to cup her firm ass and pull her tighter against me as I explored her mouth with my tongue. Then taking a deep breath, I pulled back just enough to whisper against her lips, "I want you, God, I want you, but not in a truck."

"If I invite you in, that doesn't mean I like you. I still might want to buy you a toaster for your bathtub." She lowered her mouth to my ear and nibbled. Her words were funny, but I couldn't laugh because her actions were driving me crazy.

"I'll make you like me. But until then, fine."

"Then come inside." London reached for my door handle and pulled.

I slid my legs out, London still holding on to me. She wrapped her legs around my waist and lowered her mouth back to mine as I stood up from the truck.

I felt my cock twitch at the mere thought of what it would feel like sinking into London and I had to grit my teeth and find some resolve to move forward, slowly, following the pathway that led to the front of her house. She continued pressing kisses along my jawline, down my neck, and then back up as I tried to balance the both of us and make my way up the few stairs to her front door. Jesus, I deserved a fucking award for this, she smelled so good, and all I wanted to do was to say *fuck going inside* and then put her up against the porch and take her right here. Moving my legs took a whole lot of determination.

Her arms around my neck tightened.

The lighting of the porch was enough for me to see her throat making waves. Her eyes were soft, and her flushed cheeks were tomato red. It was the very expression I had seen on women, hell, I'd put it on women after a night of great sex, and tonight, I was going to put it on her.

"Am I gonna be an old maid?" London looked up at me, and at that moment there was a clear pleading in her eyes. She needed assurance of her beauty.

I let her slide down my body until her feet were back on solid ground and then cupped her cheeks in my hands. "No, sweetheart, you definitely will not be an old maid. You are much too desirable."

"Okay," London murmured and pressed her lips to mine again. Somehow, I was eleven years old again and seeing London for the first time. She was the most beautiful girl I'd ever seen. She had also been my first school crush, but she never had time for me, never spoke to me.

When she broke the moment and stepped back, I regained my thoughts and my words. "London, where are your keys?" I lifted one brow.

"In my side pocket." She punched out her hip as if that would make this job easier. But she was wearing a dress, fuck, I didn't even know that dresses had pockets.

"Okay, can you give them to me?"

"No. You get them. You're Braden McManus, you're used to getting into a girl's pants." London laughed at her joke, and I saw the challenge in her eyes. "Don't you frisk women in your day to day job?"

She wanted to play that way, fine. "Turn around, ma'am,

you have the right to remain silent unless you are shouting my name in ecstasy, then, of course, I'll go easy."

"Easy or soft?" London giggled as she complied.

Thrusting my pelvis against her as I pressed her against her front door, I asked, "Does this feel soft to you?"

She shook her head, and I leaned in closer to her.

"Remember that anything you say can and will be used against you to prolong your torture before I finally allow you to orgasm."

Groaning, I wrapped one hand around her waist, slid my hand into her pocket, and fidgeted until I could grip the ring and pull them out. Just as I was almost clear of her pocket, she stopped me.

"Braden McManus, you were just feeling me up." London cracked up laughing and then let go of my wrist.

"London Kelly, you're gonna have a lot more than my hand if you don't hurry the fuck up and open this door." I held out her keys to her.

She was still giggling as she unlocked her door, and I reached over her head to grab the edge and hold it open.

I followed London into the kitchen, where she grabbed several bottles of beer before leading me down a hall. She was quiet, so I was assuming her sisters still lived here and she didn't want to wake them.

The second I stepped into London's bedroom, my dick was hard again, I wanted to toss her into the middle of the bed and have my way with her sweet body.

3

LONDON

Trying to ignore my conscience, which was trying to remind me that I'd never had a one-night stand before, I focused on the fact that I wanted this.

I wanted Braden.

I'd been caught up in this flutter of attraction from the moment that I first laid eyes on him earlier this evening, and with every second that had passed the feelings only intensified.

Handing him a bottle of Yuengling, I snagged one for myself and twisted the top off.

"You all right?" He looped his arm around my waist, and I found myself leaning closer and closer to him. I just liked the feel of his body next to mine, strong and gentlemanly.

"I'm great." I took several long sips off my bottle as I tried to slow my racing heart and give him the occasional fluttering of my eyelashes. I had no clue whether I was being flirtatious which was what I was going for or whether I looked like I had something caught in my eye. He grinned at me as his eyes flicked to my mouth for the briefest of moments. Ahhh yes, definitely flirtatious.

I turned and sat my bottle down on my bedside table, he did the same.

"If you don't want this to go any further, please tell me now." He traced his thumb along my bottom lip, but he didn't move a muscle to take him toward my door. He just stood there.

So, I leaned in a bit more, finally closing the distance between us until I could feel his hard cock pressed against me. "I want this, you should probably kiss me," I murmured, and I leaned in and planted a kiss on his surprised mouth. When I pulled back, he flashed me a panty-dropping grin and claimed my mouth again. His tongue delved into my mouth, and one of his hands slid to the small of my back, drawing my body against his and sending an explosion of shivers down my spine.

I pulled him over to my bed and collapsed, pulling him down on top of me.

Never in a million years did I think I would be the kind of woman who would be making the first move, being the aggressor, but his mouth on mine, his skin against my own —it was more intoxicating than any of the beer I'd had this evening, and I wanted more.

I caught his hand and led him to my breast. It was all the encouragement he needed before his hands were moving hungrily over my body. His lips moved to my neck, and I tipped my head back, inviting him to do more. The blood in my veins was boiling with desire, my body aching for him in a way it hadn't ached for anyone in a long time. I didn't know what specific alchemy Braden had going for him, but it seemed to mesh perfectly with mine. I slid my hand down his body until my palm cupped his steel-hard erection through his jeans.

Holy hell.

"I think I need you inside me right now," I murmured into his ear, wondering where this dirty-talking demon had come from all of a sudden. Maybe she had been in me all along, waiting for an excuse to come busting out. He planted a soft kiss on my mouth, hand tracing the shape of my face, my neck, and my shoulder as he looked at me.

"Are you sure?" he asked, eyes searching mine as his hand continued traveling down the slope of my waist, over my hips, and down my thigh.

"Hell, yes." I grinned, and I rolled him over so that he was underneath me and swiftly kicked off my shoes, then wiggled so I could slip my panties down my legs. I still had my dress on when I straddled him. "Please tell me you have a condom." I planted my hands on his chest and began grinding my bareness against his jeans. His eyes had darkened with need for me, and a flutter of satisfaction rolled through me.

"I do." He patted my thigh, signaling for me to get up, and when I rolled over, he quickly got up and then pulled his shirt off, dropped it to the floor, and then reached into his pocket for a condom. Trying to slow my breathing, I watched as he unfastened his belt and allowed his pants to drop to the ground, then let his briefs follow. His dick sprang free, and for a second, I just wanted to stare at it. Maybe it was the alcohol talking, but his dick was beautiful. I licked my lips and followed his movements as he sheathed himself and slid onto the bed next to me. Good god, the man was nothing but temptation, and I was completely unable to resist climbing on top of him.

Braden laid back on the bed and pulled me over on top of him and then pulled my face to his, our lips locking, his tongue sweeping inside my mouth. Every breath he exhaled sent tiny shivers all over my skin. While lost in the kiss, I straddled him, his fingers softly digging into my thighs as he massaged my upper legs and moved to cup my ass. Not breaking our kiss, his fingers dug into my hips. and he squeezed. It took me a second to realize that he was trying to lift me, but when I did, I let him guide me so that he could position his cock at my entrance. Closing my eyes, I held my breath as I lowered myself onto him, and both of us let out matching groans of relief as I did so.

He wrapped his arms around me, and I heard a zip, then felt him gathering my dress as he pulled it over my head. Feeling a little like a contortionist, I unclasped my bra and dropped it to the floor.

"Holy fuck, you're beautiful." His words were little more than a growl as he wrapped both hands around my waist and began lifting me up and then letting me slide back down his long shaft. I had forgotten how good it felt to be *wanted* like this, to be with someone who seemed to want me and only me—the power it imbued in me, how gorgeous it made me feel. I leaned forward and kissed him deeply, moaning as one of his hands sank into the back of my hair to trap me there.

Not that I would complain.

The two of us were entwined like that for what felt like forever—him moving up into me, me moving down against him. We fell into a pace like we'd been built to go together this way. Our bodies seemed to fit so perfectly, our mouths a dance that didn't misstep.

Sweat bloomed all over my body as the pleasure started to build deep inside me, and he slowed his thrusts, going deep and long as his fingers tugged my hair a bit tighter. The cascade of sensation drew one last groan from between my lips, and finally, I pressed my forehead into his neck and let the pleasure take control of me. It wiped my brain clear, letting me fall into blissful nothingness for a moment. A few seconds later, his body tensed, a deep shudder ran across his whole system, and he found his release deep inside me.

We slowly unfurled from each other, and he got up and disposed of the condom while I took several long, slow swallows of beer. I was too exhausted to decide if what I had just done had been a bad idea, and frankly, I didn't care, so when I finished off my drink, I snuggled under the covers relishing in the fact that I was thoroughly satiated. I was going to turn my mind off...any moment it was going to turn off, yep, any moment now. Come on, it wasn't as if I could take it back if I regretted it now.

Plus, someone, even if it had only been for a few hours, had wanted me, had made me feel beautiful and desirable, and that was a decent salve for my wounds, at least for the time being.

After a moment, the bed shifted as he climbed in next to me. I half-turned, already dozing off, and he planted a kiss on my bare shoulder.

"Get some sleep," he whispered. "You need it."

I dozed off, satisfied and with all my worries over the ranch, my sadness of Dad's death, and the uncertainty of my future quieted.

My head was throbbing, the light was too damn bright, and someone had just let the University of Florida's marching band into my house. "Oh my god, I feel like shit."

"You look like shit too."

Twisting my aching neck toward where the sound was coming from, I saw my sister Holland standing in the doorway.

"What time is it?" I moved to sit up, which wasn't the brightest idea since it made my stomach roll, but I needed to move the cattle and get them to the back field. That was when I realized I was naked.

Oh, shit.

Braden.

I clutched my sheet and glanced to the other side of my bed. It was empty.

His clothes were also gone.

When did he leave? I had no idea.

"Why'd you wake her up? I told you to let her sleep." Paris moved into my room and sat on the bed next to me. "Just rest, I put a bottle of water and some aspirin on your nightstand."

Did you drink all of these?"

I cracked one eye open to see what in the hell Paris was talking about, shit, she was picking up several bottles of beer. I had no memory of drinking that many, but I must have. Maybe between my first and second orgasm, or was it between the second and third? Fuck.

"Why does she get to sleep? When I come home drunk, you make me get up and then shove greasy bacon in my face."

I held up one hand to get Holland to shut the hell up. Just the thought of food made me want to vomit.

"That's because you were in the habit of coming home drunk. I've never seen London drunk. And besides," Paris lowered her voice as if that would make me less likely to throw up, "greasy food is hangover food, everyone knows that."

"Sweetie, just sleep it off. Holland's already fed the horses, and Wally and I moved the cattle."

"Thank you." I knew that it took them longer to do their

chores without my help, but I appreciated it. I grabbed one of my pillows and threw it over my face to help block the sunlight streaming in through my windows.

"Ask her about the hot guy."

"I can hear you, Holland, no need for Paris to ask me, you idiot." I didn't need to open my eyes to know that Holland was flipping me the bird. "And stop flipping me off. And don't stick your tongue out."

"Admit it, Holland, we both got your number." Paris laughed.

"Whatever, just tell me about the damn guy."

"How about we let her sleep and she can tell us when she wakes? London, Holland, and I are going to run up and get your truck, we'll be back shortly."

I gave them a thumbs-up and then waited for the sound of the door to click shut before tossing the pillow aside and snatching the folded piece of paper from the far nightstand. It hadn't been there last night, and I was willing to bet neither of my sisters had seen it.

If they had, they would have asked me about it.

It was little more than a torn scrap of paper, and on it were two words: *I'm sorry.*

No salutation, no goodbye, no offer to see me again. Just "I'm sorry."

Sorry for what? For leaving me without saying goodbye? Sorry for waking me and going a second round? Sorry for driving me home in the first place? What? What the hell was he sorry for?

Staring at those words, my blood began to boil. Braden fucking McManus hadn't changed one bit in all these years. He was still a love 'em and leave 'em kind of guy. Well, fuck that, he could at least have had the decency to say goodbye, thanks, you were awesome, or see you around. But noooo, he snuck out in the middle of the night. Well, the early morning like the two-bit asshole that he was...always had been.

I crumpled the note and tossed it aside before downing two aspirin and chugging half the bottle of water. I was too pissed to go back to sleep, so I pulled on clothes and then sat on the side of my bed to pull on my cowboy boots.

People around here called them shit-kickers. And until recently, I'd never given the name cowboy boots much thought, but this morning if someone were to ask me what I'd call them, I think that something more along the lines of, good-god-are-you-fucking-kidding-me-not-again   boots. Because, let's face it, that pretty much summed up my life.

Our house was like a wagon wheel with the center being the living room and kitchen. The hallways broke off like spokes, taking you to different wings of the house, each of us had our own wing so, even though we lived together, we had our own privacy and space. It hadn't always been like that. When I was little, there were just two spokes: the one to my parents' room and the one to our rooms. Then, when we got older, Daddy decided that he needed to hear less fighting over the bathroom.

Holland and Paris were back from getting my truck and standing in the kitchen. Holland stared at me with her arms crossed. "Well, well, look what the cat drug in."

"Bite me."

"No, thanks, I'm afraid that I might get alcohol poisoning. You gonna spill about that hot guy that brought you home?"

"He went to school with Paris and me. He was in my class. His name is Braden Fucking—"

"Well now, I thought that I'd make some cookies and we could take them by the sheriff's station as a thank you.

Marcus came by to check on you this morning, he said that you were with a deputy, so I'm assuming he was the one responsible for bringing you home and that he works out of the old school building."

"If you already knew who he was, why bother asking me?" I huffed, but she just gave me a look that told me I should have known better. "Fine. If you bake them, then you can take them. I'm not going near that man. Braden McManus is an asshole. Besides, we don't have time to be coddling some deputy. We have work to do. I'm going to grab something to eat, and then I've got payroll to do."

"Hmmm, did you feel that way last night before he made you orgasm?" Paris giggled.

"Shut up, don't mention last night, it was a mistake."

"Wow, a mistake. Did you hear that, Paris?" Holland clapped one hand on Paris's back. "London made a mistake and accidentally fell on some man's dick. At least he made her happy if the noise from her room was any indication."

"Shut up, both of you."

Paris laughed. "Or was it a mistake as in you totally were unprepared and forgot to shave your legs and he was shocked that you looked like a Wooly Mammoth?"

"If you finally shaved your legs, please tell me that you at least donated it to locks of love?" Holland giggled.

"Shut up, both of you."

"Okay, okay." Paris held up her hands in surrender. "I covered a plate of fried chicken with some aluminum foil for you; it's in the oven."

"Thank you. At least I know that there is one sister worth keeping." I blew Holland a kiss as I strode off since I intended it to be more or less a kiss-off.

"And I'm going to go ahead and bake those cookies because I know you will change your mind. Daddy didn't raise us to be rude, especially not to deputies, so I know it will weigh heavy on your heart if you don't say thank you."

That last thing Braden would get from me was any kind of gratitude.

Holland sided up to her. "Well played, well played, Machiavelli."

Machiavelli, indeed. Damn manipulator was more like it. I grabbed my plate and then headed to my office to get some work done.

I SLIPPED the cheque-folio back into my desk and picked up the envelopes to hand to the guys. We paid them on the first and fifteenth of each month no matter the day. After Dad passed away, that hadn't changed. The thing that did was the number of checks I wrote. Three of our work hands quit the day after the funeral. They had been under them assumption that we wouldn't be able to handle the place and claimed it was a family decision. They lived paycheck to paycheck, and if something happened, it would devastate them. So, to get ahead of any failure on my and my sister's part, they found new jobs. I understood the family reasoning, but I didn't understand them not having faith in us. Between Paris, Holland, and I, we knew every inch of this place and how to run every damn bit of it.

As I walked out to the great room, I hollered for my sisters, "It's four o'clock."

"Duhhh, I learned how to tell time in kindergarten. I'm all grown up." Holland never could give a simple okay or yes.

"You don't act like it."

"Sorry, I was just taking the bread out of the oven to cool

while we were gone." Paris slid her apron over head and set it down. She already had her boots on and was ready.

The three of us headed out to the stables.

"Don't look now, but it's a knight on a white horse—"

"More like a jackass," Holland said, interrupting Paris.

"Well, if you'd have let me finished, then you'd know I was going to say knight on a white horse—oh, sorry, my bad...that's Gaston on Ryan."

I laughed. The three of us were totally different, but we always had agreed on one thing: our mutual dislike for Ryan Cardenas. And the problem was, Ryan wasn't a bad guy. He just got on our nerves. He was two years older than I was and had started working here when he was seventeen. From day one, the boy had been determined to get me to go out with him. "Blahhh."

"Hurry up." Paris tugged on my arm, nearly pulling it out of the socket.

"Will you stop? You're gonna cause a friggin' scene. Then we'll really come across as intelligent women able to run a farm. Way to instill confidence among the workers we have left."

"When will you stop caring what others think?" Holland asked from behind us.

Ryan had ridden past while we argued and had already dismounted and was waiting for us at the stables.

"Afternoon, ladies. Missed you this morning, London." Ryan tipped his cowboy hat.

"I wasn't feeling well."

"More like sleeping it off. That's what you get for staying up all night with that hot guy." Holland inched her way behind Ryan and then gave me a wide smile. She wanted to aggravate Ryan, but all it ever did was make him increase his attention.

Ryan wasn't bad looking. In fact, he had this rugged handsomeness about him. He kept his dirty blond hair down to his shoulders, and he would tie it back with a piece of black leather.

"Really?" Ryan's eyes brightened as he neared me. "Someone you're serious about?"

"I don't think that we need to discuss that."

"But he was hot," Paris added.

"How would you know?" I turned on her.

Holland giggled. "He sounded hot. Plus, he's a sheriff's deputy."

"Yeah, he must be a speeding ticket because he had *fine* written all over him," Paris said and then doubled over laughing at her own stupid joke.

"You two are idiots. Ryan, here's your paycheck." I handed him his envelope. "When y'all are ready, I'll be in the stables saddling up Madam Mim." I headed off, ready to see my baby, who was probably pissed since I didn't ride her this morning. Mim was a Bay Quarter horse, and her mom had been my very first horse. God, how I had loved her too.

"London, wait up." Ryan's callused fingers wrapped around my wrist, and I turned my gaze down to his hand.

"Is there something you needed, Ryan?"

He released his hold but not immediately, which pissed me off.

Idiot.

"So, when are you going to go out with me?"

"I'm not. You work for me."

"Oh, come on, let's be honest, you write the paychecks. I've been running this ranch for years."

I took several deep breaths, counted to five, and then glared at him.

"I think that my signing your check means that I'm your boss."

At that, I strode into the stable. Something about the stables was soothing. I figured it was the combination of leather, hay, and horses that seemed to encase me. When I was little and got mad, I used to run away from home. I never got much farther than the barn, where I'd curl up on a bale of hay until my temper calmed or whatever was bothering me faded. I needed to remember that, especially whenever I had to deal with Ryan, maybe I should just make all meetings with Ryan in the barn.

I stopped and grabbed two apples out of the bag on my way to see Mim. With the exception of taking care of her, I didn't really get out to the stables much anymore, which was such a shame.

"Hello, darling, did you miss me?" Her energy was wild, and she was neighing and ready to let go of some steam. "Here, take this." I handed her the apple and turned to the gorgeous black stallion that had stuck his head out of his stall next to Mim's. "Hello, Balthazar, don't worry, I brought one for you too." I handed him the second apple.

"You know that all the other horses realize that you only give your horse and Dad's horse apples? That's probably why none of them listen to you." Holland picked up the bag and handed an apple to each horse as she walked down the middle aisle of our barn.

"That's your job. I don't have to deal with them. Remember, it was you who convinced Dad that we needed more than six horses and that he should build an entire stable so you could run it and teach riding lessons and board horses. I was fine just having my ranch."

"He did it for *all* of us. He wanted it to be all three of

ours. If it was just mine, he would have named it Holland Stables and not Iron Horse."

"But he thought that he was being cheeky when he came up with that name since the symbol for Iron is Fe and it was going to be a female-run stable. Hey, if you want to take over all the financial shit, you and I can switch jobs. Remember that my job is more than just the books, which includes payroll and budgets. I also have to keep track of the monthly forage balance sheets to make sure that we are yielding enough for the cattle and the horses."

I held out my hand ready to shake on a deal.

"Not on your life, these are my babies. I'll keep my job, and you can keep yours."

"Fine. Then stop bitching." I gave Balthazar one last rub and then stepped inside Mim's stall to brush her coat and then saddle her up as Holland did the same for her own horse.

When we were done, we led them out to where Paris and Wally were waiting astride their horses. Ryan and Jack—our other field hand—were standing off to the side, clearly listening to what Paris and Wally were talking about as they saddled up horses for each of them to ride.

The ranch was four hundred acres, two-thirds a mile in all directions. We had just over one hundred beef cows, and twice a day, we moved them from one pasture to the other. Each pasture had different grass that offered different nutrients as well as variety. We'd ride out together and then split up so we could each take point to drive the cattle from one field to the next. We only had to get a few going, and then the rest would follow, but if one strayed, the rest would follow, so we had to pay attention.

When we got to the edge of the field, I broke off and Ryan followed, ugh.

"So, who was he?" Ryan rode up alongside me.

"Umm, none ya. As in none of ya business."

"I've never heard your sisters tease you about a guy, he must be something more. But why him and not me?"

Damn it. Christ on a cracker, here we go again.

I couldn't imagine myself getting involved with him romantically because he does absolutely nothing for my libido, but telling him that would probably just hurt his fragile male ego, so I kept it to myself.

Ryan's eyes were still focused on me as he pulled the horse he was riding in front of Mim and forced her to stop.

"I'm not getting into this with you again. I've told you that I'm not interested. My dad valued you and all that you did on the farm, and I know that Wally thinks the world of you. So please don't put me in this position again."

Ryan was quiet as I dug my heels into Mim, urging her to back up so that we could ride around him. I was probably the first woman who had refused him, and that was why he was so determined to have me say yes.

4

BRADEN

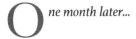ne month later...

"DUDE! You've been spacing out all morning."

I looked down at my watch to find that it was two a.m., so I guessed it was technically morning. David, a fellow deputy, was several years younger than I was and part of my East District division. There were only a few of us, so we used a room in the old school building as our main office. The other rooms in the building were used by the community for Boy Scouts, Brownie Troops, and playgroups, but it was a lot more convenient than having to drive all the way across town to the main office. Plus, it was always nice seeing kids and families.

I sighed.

It was Monday. I wanted to be home. No, scratch that, I wanted to go by the Kelly Ranch, which was what I'd wanted to do for the past month.

I hadn't been able to get her off my mind. I knew

skipping out on her was horrid, but damn, the moment I had woken up and looked at her, I hadn't known what else to do. She was all innocent, and I was Dick Dastardly and Muttley combined. I'd taken advantage of her when she was vulnerable and intoxicated all because I allowed the wrong head to do the thinking.

"Got something on your mind?"

"Obviously, but it's none of your business." Nope. I was not talking about personal shit with a coworker.

"Looks like you've got girl problems. I just hate seeing my lieutenant floundering. Let me know if you need some pointers. I'm always willing to help the less fortunate." David grinned.

"Fuck you—"

"Seminole County, signal twenty-five, reported in field off State Road 46 near Lake Harney." The radio crackled as dispatch rattled off information. "Caller was not sure of address. FD in route. All units responding twelve Charlie, 02:13 hours."

"This is eleven-eighteen," I gave dispatch my call sign, then told them that I was on my way along with David. "I'm ten fifty-one from East District substation, with fourteen-twelve."

"Seminole County copies, 02:14 hours, copy."

London lived right off Lake Harney road and State Road 46.

After jumping into my Ford Explorer, I cranked the ignition and hit my lights before pulling out of the parking lot at full speed. I didn't want to turn the sirens on unless I had to since it was the middle of the night and noises carried in the country. As I got close, I could see lights up ahead. David was behind me, but I needed to know if this was London's property and if they were awake and safe, so I reached for my radio.

"This is Seminole County, Braden McManus, do we have an ID on the address or property owner?"

"Hey, Braden, this is Ben Stinson, we are working to get it contained. No homes appear to be in danger, but from the fence, I'm guessing that this is part of the Kelly Ranch."

My heart picked up speed at those words. "What do you mean by the fence?"

"The Kelly Ranch has iron horses on the top of their fence posts."

"Has anyone notified the family of the fire yet?"

"Not yet, we're trying to take care of this, I'd guess this is their back pasture."

"No worries, I'll go there now."

"Thanks, man."

As I turned onto the side road, a pit grew in my stomach. On top of delivering the bad news to London, this would also be the first time I would see her since that night.

She had every right to hate me, and that wasn't going to get any better after I told her what I was here to tell her.

Each footstep I took up the steps felt like a thousand pounds and echoed like a clap of thunder. Taking my Stetson off, I held it under one arm and then rang the bell. Law enforcement visits in the early morning hours weren't a good thing, ever. Whether it was the accident of a loved one or just delivering bad news like I was about to do no one ever answered the door with a smile on their face.

I stood a little straighter when I saw a shadow move behind the curtains to my left. I squinted preparing for the flip of the porch light so that whoever was there could see me. When it came on, I heard the rustling and hollering.

"London, Holland, wake up. London, Holland!"

The door opened, and I was face to face with who had to be Paris.

"What's wrong?" Paris reached for my hand and pulled me inside. I glanced toward where the sound of running footsteps was coming from and found London, hair disheveled, eyes wide, running to me.

"What's wrong?" London asked, repeating her sister's earlier question.

"Ladies, there's been a fire in your back pasture, and the fire department is already there and has it under control."

"Which pasture?" London stood stock still, and she seemed to be staring through me.

"Your field that is closest to the State Road, the farthest east section."

"Oh shit, that's our hybrid field." London turned to face her sisters and said something to them that I couldn't hear.

"Thank you for telling us, Deputy. We'll head down there now."

"You can stay here and someone from the fire department will come up and talk to you once they have it contained."

"Fuck that, we're going over there." The one I was guessing to be Holland since I knew it wasn't London and she wasn't who answered the door was the first one to race off.

"I can escort you over there if you want to go, but it is cordoned off for safety reasons. You'll have to stay back."

London didn't say a word before she turned and ran back down the hallway that I knew all too well led to her bedroom. Paris ran off as well. Less than five minutes later, all three women were ready.

"Here." I held open the door to my cruiser.

"We've got it," London snapped, and the three of them piled into her truck ready to follow me.

Arriving on scene, I jumped out before London could get her door open. "You three need to wait here until someone gives the all-clear."

I looked at London, but she wasn't meeting my eyes.

"Let me find out some info." I walked back toward my truck and then spoke into my radio. "Ben, this is Braden, I have the owners of the Iron Horse Stables with me."

The radio crackled. "Where are you?"

"We're parked behind truck thirty-seven."

"I'll be over as soon as I can."

By the time I headed back, David was already talking to the girls. "They have the fire under control. They called in a helicopter, it just left. Our biggest fear is it spreading, and we just need to watch it. This is prime burn area, and with the Lake Harney subdivision so close, we couldn't take any chances of the fire getting out of hand."

Trying to offer some information, I added, "The helicopter bucket drops about eighteen-hundred gallons."

"Is that true?" What the fuck? Of course it was true. I didn't just make that shit up. I just said it, why would I lie? But London directed her question to David so I turned to him too, raising my eyebrow as I waited for his answer.

David looked at me a little apprehensively. "Yes."

"Ladies, it's going to be a while, so if you want to go home, I can come get you or call you when they are done here?" I offered. "Like I mentioned, someone from the fire department will come and talk to you."

"No, we'll stay. Is that okay with you, David?"

"Yes?" David looked at me for confirmation, so I nodded.

"Then why don't you let me turn your truck around so you three can sit on the tailgate while you wait?" I held out my hand. I could see London warring with her thoughts on whether she was going to ignore me on this as well or not. I wanted to smirk, but I knew that would only make things worse.

"I'll turn the truck around, be right back," London said to Paris, and Holland, as she strode off. When she got back, I moved to stand next to her and fought to hold back a laugh when she took a step sideways.

"Hey, Braden." I looked up to see Ben.

"Hey, Ben, have you met London, Paris, and Holland Kelly?"

"You don't need to make introductions," London murmured under her breath as if she were annoyed.

"We know each other." Ben nodded to each of the sisters. "My daughter takes riding lessons from Holland."

I felt stupid, she was right I didn't need to do introductions, but she could have said they knew each other. "I'm sorry about all of this, but the fire is out. Right now, we are just watching for any hot spots. As soon as we feel that the area is secure, we will be able to examine the extent of the damage."

"I don't get it. We aren't in a drought or having wildfires, do you have an idea of what caused this?" London held a sister's hand in each of hers.

"Honestly? Our temperature gauge was going off," Ben explained. "It was telling us that the fire was hotter than normal."

Paris let out a gasp. "Chemical?" We all looked at her in shock that she knew this. "I watch *Chicago Fire*."

"Yes, that's a possibility, but we won't know until we test the area. Let me get back over there and check on everything. I'll be back as soon as I have new info."

Ben walked off, and I turned to London. "What do you

want to do now? You want to go up to the house and wait for me to call you? It could take a few more hours before they clear all the hot spots."

"Yeah, we better. I need to figure out about the cattle." London shoved one hand through her hair.

"I'll call Asher, he'll tell us what we need to do," Paris assured her.

"Just have Ben come up and give us any info when he's done." London held out one hand to shake mine as if we were done.

I didn't think so. We were not going to leave it there. I unclipped my cellphone from my belt and handed it to London. "Why don't you enter your number so I can call you if anything changes." I tilted my head, silently daring her to refuse the phone.

When she snagged the device from my hand, I fought back my grin. Even in all of this shit going on, London was a bright spot. After she handed it back, I immediately pressed call. When her phone rang, I grinned. "Now you have mine as well."

I waited until they drove off, then headed over to David.

"Wow, she's pissed at you."

"You think?"

"What did you do to her?"

"I'm not discussing this with you." I lifted my Stetson so I could wipe the sweat from my brow and gave me an excuse to not meet David's stare. What the fuck? I was his boss, and for some reason, I was the one who felt like I was about ready to get reprimanded. "I'm going to go see if Ben has any new information, he's standing near the edge."

I took my time walking over there, and when I came to a stop next to him, I asked, "Any thoughts?"

"I'd bet my next paycheck that someone started this fire."

"It's next to the main road, is there a chance it was some random driver who happened to throw out their lit cigarette?" God knows we'd had plenty of those start fires over the years, but only when it was an extreme drought.

"That's always a possibility, but it wouldn't raise the temperature. You need an accelerant to do that. The fire investigator will be here at eight. We'll get a better idea then."

"Any clue on damage?"

"I'm not sure how their pastures are divided, but this one is wiped out, the fire jumped the northwest fence line and started on the next field, but we caught it, I would say less than an acre of that field is gone." Ben pointed toward the area he was referring to.

Nearly twenty-five years ago most of this area was ravaged by fires that swept across the state. I understood why Ben and his crew weren't taking any chances, with our lack of rain lately, keeping all of the nearby pastures and woods heavily soaked would be vital to help prevent this from tuning into an all hands on deck catastrophe.

It was just past five, when Ben gave me the word that he felt confident that the fire was truly controlled. My shift was over in an hour, but I didn't want to go home, I didn't want to leave London.

"I'm heading up to the house now to relay the news. Holler if you need me."

"Will do." Ben gave me a mock salute and headed back off in full turnout gear to check on his team.

After waving goodbye to David, I jumped into my Sheriff's Department Explorer and drove off. Driving down the gravel road to their house and hearing all of my equipment rattle, I made a mental note to help them grade this road. I had no clue when the last time they'd had dragged a tractor across it, but the ruts were so bad that I'd be shocked if their vehicles were still in alignment.

When I pulled up to the house, the truck wasn't there, so I followed the path down to the barn and climbed out. London was talking to three men along with her sisters, so I hung back until she was done and made her way over to me. Her sisters joined us, but the three men didn't move, so I eyed them, London turned and gave me the go-ahead to speak in front of them.

"That pasture, how many acres is it?" I pulled out my notepad and began taking notes.

London crossed her arms but didn't speak.

Paris answered, "That one is about, eighty—more or less."

"And what about the field to the northwest?"

"That's the largest." Holland chimed in, but I kept my eyes focused on London. "It's about one hundred fifty acres."

"Your big field did sustain some damage, but it was mild, maybe an acre or so, that's just a guess. The pasture next to the main road was totally wiped out."

London's arms tightened across her body, her nails dug into her arms, but she kept silent.

"The investigator will be out here soon to test for an accelerant and arson."

"Arson?" Holland's face was a mask of fury. "You mean someone deliberately burned our fields?"

"That's what we're going to look for."

"The cattle?" London asked and then looked to Paris as if she might have the answer.

"Don't worry, Asher will be here soon and we're going to

test all the fields. We can't have the cattle grazing until we know what's going on," Paris assured her.

Just then, two trucks pulled up the driveway and parked. Marcus got out of the first one, and his brother, Asher, followed. A twinge of jealousy hit me over the way London flew into Marcus's arms. "Shh, we're going to get the cattle moved," Marcus crooned.

I averted my gaze and saw Paris wrapped in Asher's arms. I wasn't sure why Marcus was here, but I totally understood Asher's presence. He was the local large animal veterinarian and was probably here to check on the herd.

"Paris was just telling me that you guys suspect arson. She and I are going to head out to the pasture that wasn't burned, I just want to take a few grass cuttings and run some litmus tests on it. I'm assuming it will all be fine since whatever chemical was used should have burned off in the fire, but it's better to be safe than sorry. I just don't want them ingesting a ton of chemical laden ash. Why doesn't someone go and speak to the new neighbor and see if he wouldn't mind allowing the cattle to graze for a bit. His farm is almost twice this size," Asher instructed.

"I'll do that," a man about my age said. He was wearing a black T-shirt, worn jeans, and boots. He turned to me, and something in his eyes bothered me. "I'm Ryan, I run the ranch."

I cut my eyes to London, who looked as if she were ready to throw down. "Excuse me? Since when? Last I knew, I ran this ranch along with my two sisters."

"Sorry, London, I just meant that I'm the foreman of the ranch." Ryan turned so that London couldn't see him and gave me a mocking wink.

I hated when men were condescending to women, and unfortunately, it was something I saw more often than not.

We had a ton of good ole boys who believed women should be barefoot and pregnant while in the house making them a sandwich.

"Hold off there a second, Ryan. Let's see what your bosses want you to do. If they give the all clear for you to speak on their behalf, then go ahead."

My eyes locked with London's, and she was fighting back a smile.

"Ryan, you can go and ask if our new neighbor will let the cattle graze in his pastures, but take Wally with you. And Ryan? Please remember who owns this ranch, who signs your paychecks." London didn't step away from Marcus, and that bothered me even more. "Is there anything else you need from us, Deputy McManus?"

"Braden." I was exasperating her, and a small part of me felt guilty for it. But she was giving me some attention, which was better than being ignored by her.

"Well, I'm going to go check on the horses." Holland stepped back and turned toward the stables.

"Why don't I grab the change of clothes from my truck and then help you with whatever you need. I'm off the rest of the day."

"Why don't you stay there and let us do our chores?"

London finally pulled away from Marcus and headed toward a stall, hollering over her shoulder, "Thanks, Deputy, have a great life."."Fine, I'll head home and get a nap, but I'll be back. We can talk later."

"No need, Deputy McManus."

"I beg to differ, Miss Kelly, unless of course you want to talk over everything now. I need to apologize to you, I was wrong, I shouldn't have snuck out without—"

"Will you shut up? Go do whatever you need to do.

When you come back, we will talk. Right now, I have work to do."

Oh, she was mad, and she was determined to make me suffer, but I'd regretted leaving her the second I was out her door. All I wanted was for her to listen to me, to look at me, to give me a second chance, whether I truly deserved it or not.

London went back to working in the stall, and I gave a half wave to the rest of the group as I headed for my Explorer. I was going to have to do some groveling. But truth be told, I deserved any punishment she was going to dish out. I wasn't giving up because I wanted another chance. I'd fucked up. I wouldn't be making that mistake again.

Normally, when I got home from work, I'd hit the bed and be out in no time, but not today. No, this morning I lay there staring at the fucking crack on my ceiling that I'd never noticed before and thought of London and the way her body felt when she was under me.

The way her eyes darkened to that of a well-aged brandy just before I slid into her.

I wasn't sure if I actually fell asleep or not because it seemed that I was still thinking of London when I realized that it was a quarter after ten. After jumping in the shower, I dressed in jeans, a T-shirt, and work boots before heading back to the ranch.

When I arrived, Ben was there with the fire inspector. I gave them both a chin nod and then took up a spot next to London, who was sitting next to Holland on the couch.

"From our preliminary test, it appears to have been what we classify as fuel oil number one category, which can be kerosene, charcoal starter fluid, or one of several different insecticides. The way the fire spread, I believe that whoever started it was inside the property perimeter. The fire began at the point of that field farthest from State Road 46 and then burned toward the highway. My guess is that they wanted to do damage but didn't want to damage the house. I'll let you know as soon as we hear back from the lab on the actual chemical. My team is currently combing the area around your farm and looking for any evidence."

"Such as?" London looked up at me after she'd asked the question.

"Containers like gas cans or matches, lighters, even clothing that may have been burned. I'll need a list of all the people who have access to the ranch. Also, Ben mentioned that your father recently passed, I'm sorry for your loss."

"Thank you," London and Holland whispered in unison.

"Many times after a death, there's a battle with the will, family members are upset over who will inherit. Anything like that?"

"No. My dad was an only child. It's just the three of us. We each got one-third, and we are not allowed to sell it. If one of us wants out, they must give their portion of the land divided equally between the remaining two." London reached over and squeezed Holland's hand.

"Employees or boyfriends? Pissed any of them off lately?"

"No," London said, but my mind was going to the man who was all too quick to claim responsibility for the ranch.

The inspector and Ben left just as Ryan, Paris, and Asher walked in. When Ryan saw Braden standing next to me, his face twisted into a scowl.

"I'll get some food ready. Holland want to help?" Paris headed to the kitchen.

"Not particularly."

"Do it anyway," Paris snapped, forcing Holland to come with her.

"You've got me, I'll always help," Asher announced as he followed behind. God, could the man be any more in love with my sister and could she be any more oblivious about it?

"I'm going to head out, I need to check in on my mom and then get up to the bar. Call if you need anything." Marcus kissed me on the side of my head and then hollered his goodbyes to the rest of the group. Sometimes I wished that I had feelings for Marcus. It would make life so much easier. I didn't, though.

"Thanks for going to the neighbors," I said to Ryan, who was still glaring at me, "but Asher feels that the pasture is safe."

"May we go into your office and talk about this?"

"No, it's fine, Braden can hear."

"London, I don't think we need anymore outsiders in the family business right now."

Family? He...he didn't think? What the hell?

Calm down, London, calm down. Count to ten...in Spanish. Ryan is an idiot. He's hurt, that's all. He feels that his role as foreman has been usurped since Dad passed.

"Fine. Braden, will you excuse me for a second? I'll be right back. Stay and have lunch with us, it's the least we can do."

Braden gave me a half-smile and nodded before his focus turned to Ryan and his eyes darkened. Yep, these two were going to have a cockfight, and I didn't have time for either one of their bullshit.

"Let's go, Ryan, you need to get back to work." I headed to my office with Ryan on my heels.

Ryan stepped in and moved to close the door. "Please leave the door open."

"But we have things to discuss."

"I understand that, but the only people who come down this hall are my sisters, and they have every right to hear whatever it is you want to tell me. So, if you don't mind, I said to leave the door open." Ryan swung the door back hard enough that knob hit the wall, and my anger flared. "I'm not sure what's gotten into you lately, but on top of what has happened with the field, I don't have time for your drama."

"Fine. I met our neighbor, Mr. Brooks, and he's more than willing to let the cattle on his property for a fee."

"A fee? But we're neighbors."

"He said it's business. Eighteen dollars per acre, per

month, and your crew makes sure the pasture is kept rotated."

"That's ridiculous! Eighteen dollars is the standard rate if they do everything."

"I'm just the messenger. His field closest to ours is fenced off at around one hundred ten acres."

"Let me think about it, I need to run the numbers. It might be better to just keep the cattle here and bring in some different hay for the few months it takes to regrow the Bermuda grass. I guess we won't be having any neighborly parties with the new folks, huh?"

"It's just him. He's into horse racing and does a lot of training and houses some of thoroughbreds during the winter. He said that if I needed a job I could always go there."

"Does that interest you, Ryan?"

"I'm just saying that I do a lot around here—a lot more than you realize. You'd miss me if I wasn't here, you'd feel it."

"I don't question that you're an asset to the ranch. But I can hire assets that don't give me attitude for less money. If you feel the need to go work somewhere else, be my guest." That conceited prick, he thought that I'd beg him to stay. If it weren't for the damn unemployment that I knew he'd claim or the fact that I didn't trust him not to lie about some jacked-up charges like hostile work environment or sexual harassment, I'd fire him. But, damn it, he never did anything that was hands-down, unequivocally fire-worthy, something that I could hold over him if he didn't leave peacefully.

"The cattle really need more than just the one pasture. I think that you are going to have to take Mr. Brooks up on his offer even if it is high."

"Your thoughts are noted."

When Ryan stood and finally left, I followed him out to the living room. Might as well get all the talking shit over with. "Braden, you wanted to speak with me?" I waved for him to come on back to my office.

"How long has the guy worked for you?" Braden tilted his chin toward Ryan, who had just slammed my front door.

"Too long. Fifteen years, but my dad liked him, probably because he never undermined my dad like he does me."

"Is that what he's doing, undermining you?"

"Yes. His ego is bruised. He thinks women are incapable of anything. I think he's amazed that my dad would leave a successful farm to three 'incompetent' women."

"But you aren't incompetent."

"I know that. My dad knew that. Hell, he raised us and trained us. He had us running this farm. By the time Holland was ten we each had our roles firmly identified and were working them. But Ryan doesn't see that, he only see girls standing in the way of men."

"What do you mean?" Braden stopped at the open doorway to my office and leaned against the doorframe.

"He's been asking me out since we were teenagers, and I've always said no."

"Why's that?"

"Not sure, just never really saw him as date material." Neither one of us moved into my office, we just stood there neither going in or out, neither of us making a move one way or the other. It was kind of symbolic.

"What's his last name?" Braden bit the inside of his cheek while his mind got lost on something.

"Cardenas, why?"

"I don't know, just the sheriff in me."

Why, why, why did he have to say that? Something about his sentence had my mind spiraling into the gutter and has me thinking, I'd like to have the sheriff in me. God, something was seriously wrong with me. He'd left me a damn apology, and all I wanted was to have him again. "So what did you want to talk about?"

"I owe you an apology."

"You gave it, remember? In your note it said, *I'm sorry*." I was being a total bitch but he was making me uncomfortable, I always got nervous around him. Why after all these weeks did he think I'd accept his apology? He should have done it immediately.

"Let me explain, please."

I crossed my arms and straightened my shoulders. My daddy used to call it my London-takes-on-the-world stance. He used to tell me that if anyone ever gave me trouble, all I had to do was assume that stance and I'd intimidate the hell out of them. But by the look on Braden's face, I didn't think it was working on him.

"I saw you lying there that night, you were so gorgeous, but you were totally out of it. It hit me that maybe you had been more intoxicated than I had realized, and I felt like an ass. I was embarrassed. I pride myself on my morals, and there you were so beautiful and innocent, and all I could think about was that I had taken advantage of you when you were drunk."

"I knew perfectly well what I was doing, and I fully consented, so you have no reason to feel guilty. So if that was all you wanted to talk about, I guess we're done."

"No. Let me make it up to you, please? Go out with me...on a real date."

"Umm...no. You and I are like oil and water, we don't mix." I pursed my lips, forcing myself not to show any emotion over that bold-face lie.

I stepped back when he stepped forward, I took another

step back when he advanced again, until my back was against the bookcase and his hands were pinning me in place.

"Why, London Kelly, do I think that you are lying? I think you know that we mix." He pressed his hips against mine. "We mix very well."

"Lunch is ready." Paris's voice interrupted us.

"Coming," my voice squeaked as I shouted back. After clearing my throat, I tried again. "Huh, coming, be right there."

Instead of turning and walking back out of my office like I thought he would, Braden righted himself, as in adjusted the front of his pants. Oh sure, I don't think he meant for me to notice because he turned sideways but I noticed. I noticed that ginormous bulge in the front of his jeans.

"You okay? You're blushing?" he asked, turning back to face me and then reaching up to cup the side of my face.

I pulled away. "Mm-hmm, just tired and hungry. You can stay for lunch." I raced out of my office, not wanting him to know where my mind had just been.

In the kitchen, Braden pulled out my chair at the table and sat next to me as if he was some missing puzzle piece to the familiar gathering.

"What did you make?" I looked up at Paris as she and Asher brought plates to the table.

"Calzones. I had some dough already in the fridge and sauce from spaghetti last night, so it was easy."

"Sounds awesome. Do you always cook like this?" Braden took his plate from Paris. "Thank you."

"Pretty much, it's my thing. I'd spend all day in the kitchen or in a garden if I could. That's why I'm always in charge of trying different seeds and seeing what mixes for the grass."

"Why don't you build a garden then?" Braden sounded genuinely interested in what Paris had to say, and I felt a tightening in my shoulders.

Holy hell, I was jealous, some part, a very small part of me was jealous...of my sister. No, that couldn't be. I loved my sister. I glanced over to Asher, who seemed to feel the same way I did about it.

"I don't really want to waste all that time just to have well fed deer."

"My dad and I built a garden for my mom. It isn't huge, but it's big enough for her to cook for the family and to give some to neighbors." Braden looked over to me, and I plastered on a smile. "The way it's designed, it keeps the deer and rabbits out."

"Oh, I'd love that. I know just where I'd have it built as well." I couldn't be jealous when I saw the look of happiness on my sister's face. I felt sorry for Asher, but if Braden could make Paris this happy, then who was I to stand in the way?

"Asher, are you off this weekend?" Braden turned his focus to Asher, but it was me who sucked in a sharp breath because Braden reached under the table and lightly touched my hand.

"Barring any emergencies."

"Then this weekend we will plan on building it." Really? Just because I had this tinge of jealousy, didn't mean that I'd forgiven him. Hell, he hadn't even apologized yet.

"Sometime this afternoon, I've got to run into the station and file a report about the fire and then I can come back. I can help with whatever you all need. I'm off for the next two days." Braden slid his hand up my leg and I smacked it away. He chuckled but placed it back on my thigh and ate one handed.

After lunch when Paris started clearing the dishes, I

figured that it was the perfect opportunity to get rid of Braden. "Hey, Paris, I need to talk with you, and Holland. We need to discuss some things pertaining to ranch business."

Braden turned to me and positioned his legs on either side of my chair.

"Okay, I get the hint, I'll run to the station, but I'll be back. London, you have no idea how sorry I am. I've wanted to come by so many times but had no clue what to say."

"Obviously, you still don't." I could feel the heat rising on my cheeks. "What are you most sorry for, Braden? Sorry for sleeping with me or sorry for leaving in the middle of the night?"

"Please—"

"No, please listen to me. You had your one chance, and you blew it. You don't get another. We can be friends, but we will never be anything more."

"I don't believe that, I saw how you responded to me in your office. You feel something for me."

"Well, yeah, I feel something when I see a dead squirrel on the side of the road as well. Doesn't mean I'm going to go out with it. It just means that squirrel was an idiot and didn't get out of the way fast enough." I squeezed my hands together to emphasize my point.

"Fine, you think that, and I'll accept being your friend." Braden had just given me what I had wanted, but I hadn't realized that it would feel like such a smack in the face. "For now anyway, just so you know, I fully intend to change your mind."

"No, you won't. I'm headstrong." I stood, which was a mistake because he stood with me, putting us chest to chest.

"Good, it will make the challenge that much more fun and victory that much sweeter." Braden leaned forward and placed a soft kiss on my cheek. "I'll see you in a little while."

"Listen, you and I...well, we are different. I'm not the kind of girl you usually date."

"What kind of woman do you think I usually date?" Braden's face looked stern as he stepped back and moved his hands to rest on his hips.

"You know the kind. Umm, the ones who aren't...well, the ones that are like you."

"Like me, how?"

"Don't make me say it."

"Contrary to what you believe, I'm not a man whore. That night, I freaked out—not because of what we shared but because of...because I was worried that you were going to wake up and totally regret everything. The alcohol would have worn off, your dad's funeral was over, and those emotions were going to hit you. I should have been the one to control myself around you, but damn it, you're just so fucking irresistible and the last thing that I wanted was to be the thing that you regretted."

With those words, Braden turned and strode out the door, leaving me speechless.

What was I doing? This was Braden fucking McManus. I was going to get hurt.

Paris, Holland, and I sat at the table and made a plan. After the alkaline test, Asher believed that the sod was fine. He and Paris had set up our portable irrigation system to help dilute any residue that might have remained on the open pasture. They'd also arranged for Jack, our other farm hand, to move it to a different area every two hours.

Holland had kept the horses fed and stabled all day, so there was no worry about them ingesting something they shouldn't.

"We need to talk about Ryan," I said.

"Ryan?" Holland raised one brow. "What's crawled up his ass? He's gotten worse since Dad died. I mean he's always been a dick, but now, I'm ready to buy him a cape and call him Super Dick."

"Honestly, I've no fucking clue. Today he told me how much we'd miss him if he wasn't here and that our neighbor offered him a job like that would scare me."

"I'm willing to find out whether we'd miss him or not, aren't you?" Holland asked.

"I am, but I figured that we could stop relying on him so much and start asking Wally and Jack to do more around here. Maybe Ryan will get the hint that we don't need him. I'm just not ready to terminate him. You know that he'd file something against us."

"So? Let him. We are good people, we don't mistreat our animals, and we don't use caustic pesticides." Paris's cheeks were red with fury.

"That isn't the point. The point is that we'd be under a microscope and our buyers and Holland's clients might wonder what's going on. It could do just as much damage even if we're innocent."

"Aghhh." Holland hit the table.

"Let me finish. Ryan was only one part. The other is our neighbor. He's willing to let our cattle graze on his adjoining pasture, provided we take care of all the rotation and seeding."

"That sounds fair, the cattle really should have more than our one pasture area to graze." Paris looked to Holland to get her take on the situation, but I held up my hand to stop them.

"He's willing to do it for eighteen dollars per acre per month."

"What? That's bullshit!" Holland exclaimed. "Who the hell does he think he is? Does he realize that people don't act like that around here? We help neighbors out. What does he need all that land for anyway?"

"It doesn't matter what he needs it for, it's his. He can do whatever he wants with it. Anyway, I'm going to check around and see if we can't just bring some Fescue and Bluegrass in while the other pasture regrows. I'll compare costs and see which is best. The cost will kill us, but losing the cattle will hurt more." I ran my fingers through my hair. "We are up to one hundred and two heads, and for that number of cattle, we'd need about two hundred acres to feed them for the year, but I'm guessing that it will only be six months max. So we need to decide if we are going to try to make our large pasture work and bring in hay, sell some cattle, or bite the bullet and talk to the neighbor."

"We'll make our pasture work. We have to do it," Holland demanded.

"I don't know. Technically, we need two acres per steer, and you're telling me that we are going to try to do one acre per steer?" Paris questioned. "I think you need to run the numbers, figure out how much hay we are going to need to bring in because I'm assuming that all the pasture land will be trampled and not really consumed."

I nodded. She was right. I had a lot of thinking to do. The cattle were my forte and I needed to make sure that everything ran correctly and humanely.

6

BRADEN

I searched the database for any information on Ryan Cardenas. I didn't find anything out of the norm from a typical hotheaded teenager. Male, Caucasian, age thirty-two. He'd had a few altercations as a teenager but nothing too serious. Looked like his mother passed away when he was seventeen, which was when he'd started working at the ranch. I couldn't put my finger on it, but there was something about the guy I didn't like that went above and beyond the typical jerk.

I was still trying to figure out the why of it as I climbed into my truck and pulled out of the sheriff's station. After a minute, I grabbed my phone and dialed my mom. It was our typical routine whenever I was in my car.

"Sounds like you're in your car, where are you heading?"

"Last night there was a fire, and it burned close to a hundred acres. I'm heading over to the farm to see if I can help."

My mom let out a long sigh. "You are a sweet boy, why haven't you given any girl the chance to find this out? I'm not getting any younger, I'd like to be able to play with my grandchildren."

"Okay, okay. I know, you tell me this all the time. Do you remember London Kelly?" My mom had worked in the Geneva Elementary School office for years although that wasn't the grade school I'd gone to. London and I hadn't met until middle school.

"Oh, I remember her and her sisters, that little one was a spitfire."

"Well, it was their farm that burned."

"I'm so sorry. Didn't I just read an obituary for their father?"

"Yes, he died a month ago."

"I'm glad you're helping. If they need anything, let us know. Your dad can drive out there and help."

"Thanks, Mom, love you."

"Love you too."

I disconnected and turned at the sign that said Kelly Ranch and Iron Horse Stables. The truck wasn't parked out front, so I headed to the stables.

Though when I parked and walked inside the stables, it was Ryan and not London that greeted me.

"What brings you here so soon, Deputy?"

"I'm here to speak to your boss." I fought to hold back my silent high five. Some people were so easy to rile, and Ryan was one of them.

"She and her sisters are out riding the perimeter. I'll tell her you stopped by. Do you have a card or something that I can give her?"

"Nah, I'll wait, this isn't official business. Don't let me keep you, go back doing whatever London and the girls have you working on for them."

"I'm not working on anything for them. I'm doing what it

takes to keep our ranch going. It is a working ranch and requires nonstop care, more than what the girls even know."

"Your ranch? Maybe I'm confused, but I thought that Samuel left it to his daughters."

"Yeah, well...London and I have been together since she was fifteen, so it's almost like it's mine. I feel like it's home." Ryan pulled his shoulders back so that he stood a little taller.

"Hmmm, interesting."

"So, as I was saying, why don't you just leave me your card, and I'll give London the message."

"And as I mentioned earlier, I'll wait and keep you company. You can tell me all about you and London and how this ranch is part yours." I watched as the scowl on the man's face deepened, and it was that look that fueled me to keep adding gasoline to the fire already inside him.

"I don't know what you're playing at, but you have no chance with London."

Interesting that he picked that as his response. Normally, I wasn't one to poke at people, but I wanted at this guy, he made it so easy.

"Well, I won't keep you from doing your work. I'm going to go find London."

Heading back outside, I was met by beauty...that was the best way to describe her. London was astride her horse and was galloping toward us with her sisters flanking her.

London pulled her horse to a halt, and I stepped up to give her a hand. I think that she took it to appease me because she clearly didn't need help handling her horse.

"So you did come back." London's smile was hesitant, as if she was amazed that I'd returned.

"I told you that I would. I said that I was coming to help. You aren't going to scare me off so easily, London."

68   DANIELLE NORMAN

"Really? You came to help?" London looked surprised. "What's the catch?"

"No catch. I'm free labor. Well, I may bum dinner off you."

"I think we can manage that."

I followed her as she led her horse into the stable.

"Let me get Mim brushed, and then we can get working."

I was listening to what London was saying as she went through the chores on her list.

"I need to call around about getting on a regular delivery for hay as well as soy and grain for the cattle until we can get the pasture regrown. Also sometime over the next day or so, I need to make sure that the old pole barn is cleared out so that we have a place to store all of it. Jack has the overseer hooked to the tractor and is spreading out a layer of seed."

"Hey—" I leaned back to see who had bumped me and was met by a long face with dark soulful eyes. The beautiful horse decided that it was the perfect time to head-butt me. Reading the name on his stall, I trailed my hand down his muzzle. "Well, hello, Jafar."

"I was wondering where I'd lost you." I looked over my shoulder to see London peeking out of a stall several down the row. "I see that you met Jafar. He's a sweetie, isn't he?"

"Yeah." I continued petting him and taking in the horses around me, Shere Khan, Gaston, Maleficent, Ursula, Hopper, Balthazar, there were several more, but I couldn't read them all from where I was standing. "What's up with the Disney villain names?"

"My first horse was named Grimhilde, the evil queen in Snow White. That was her name when my dad bought her for me. After that, we just gave every horse a villain name. Sounds weird, I know."

"A little, but I'm getting used to your weird side." I winked at her, and I'd be damned if London Kelly didn't blush.

"I'm finished with Mim. You ready?" London stood next to me.

"Bye, Jafar. You keep these other ladies in line, you hear me? If they're anything like this one"—I elbowed London—"then I'm sure you have your hands, hooves, whatever full."

The Kelly girls worked hard. Even though I'd only been there a few hours, I was exhausted and had no idea how they'd managed to keep it up all day. I gave London a peck on her cheek, promised to meet her early the next morning, and then left for home.

THE NEXT MORNING, London and I started out early, and setting up the irrigation was not easy work. Even though the sun only was just cresting the horizon on this late September day, it was already hot as hell, and we were sweating.

By the time we had the water wheels stationed, the hoses hooked, and the timers programed, it was time to move to another three acres. Every forty-five minutes, we repeated this.

I dropped off the water wheel and then drove the four wheeler out of the sprinkle zone where London and I had designated our meeting spot.

"You ready for lunch?" London asked as she looked toward the sun.

"I'm starved. Want to go after this round?"

"Nah, we can leave 'em since they are on a timer. The

machines will automatically turn off, and then we can move them after lunch."

I counted in my head; if each water wheel did three acres and this was the sixth time running, hmm. "Not bad, we already have thirty-six acres taken care of."

London let out a chuckle. "Not bad at all, Jack got thirty acres done yesterday, so we only have about twenty-four more to go before we start all over."

I groaned, as I felt every muscle in my body ache. She, however, didn't look fazed at all.

Lunch in the Kelly house was loud and full. Paris definitely embraced her role as the family cook.

"All of this for lunch?"

"Paris spoils us." The affection in London's voice was evident as she wiped off her hands. "Where's Holland?"

"No clue, she's been out most of the morning," Paris said as she handed me a platter to take to the table.

"What's for lunch?" Asher asked as he walked through the door without knocking.

"Asher Kinkaide, can you at least say hello and not just think about your stomach?" Paris chided. London said Paris and Asher were just friends, but they acted more like an old married couple.

"Hello, y'all. Now, what's for lunch?" He moved into the kitchen and washed his hands before he tousled Paris's hair.

I had just slid into a chair when Marcus strode in and made his way to the table. "Hey, Braden, nice seeing you."

"You too. You always here for lunch?" I looked back and forth between him and his brother.

"Are you kidding me? If you had a neighbor who cooked like Paris, you'd always be here too."

But our discussion halted when Holland stormed in,

slamming the door behind her so hard that the photos that hung on wall rattled.

"Mr. Brooks is a dick!" Holland's face was tomato-red, and she looked as if she was going to burst into flames any moment.

"What did he do?" London didn't get up, obviously used to her sister's tantrums.

"I was out riding the perimeter, and he rode through and just stared at me, all judge like. I know that he was just making sure we weren't using his land. Then when he saw me galloping on Shere Khan, he had the audacity to holler about the way I was riding him. That man has some balls to try to tell me how to ride."

Since no one else was going to ask, I did. "What exactly did he say?"

"I don't know. I didn't stick around to listen. I flipped him off and then Khan and I hightailed it back over here. What's worse is that the lessons area borders his front pasture, and he's always out there freaking watching me!"

"All right, Holland, just let it go." London poured some tea in Holland's glass as Paris slid food onto her plate. Holland's outrage and temper outbreaks were clearly a common occurrence in this house since no one seemed phased in the slightest.

"How's the watering going? When I'm done with my two o'clock class I can help you." Holland was clearly already over her anger.

"Thanks but there are only two wheels anyway so we've got it. Besides, after lunch I need to return a few calls from the help wanted ads that I have up on the farmer sites for ranch hands."

"Wouldn't that be better to do later, when people were

home?" I was showing my complete ignorance of the way a ranch works, and I knew it.

"Nah, most of these men get up before the crack of dawn. Some start their days as early as three if they need to get milk or eggs to a farmer's market. So since I don't know their schedules, you don't ever call a farmhouse after six in the evening, that's just proper etiquette." London shrugged her shoulders, letting me know that was just the way of the world, well, her world.

After lunch I sat in a chair, feeling like a total waste since I couldn't even continue with the irrigation having no clue how to program the system without her. I picked up a magazine off the coffee table, *The Cattlemen Association,* and leafed through it while London was back in her office. I'd finished that magazine and had moved onto *Progressive Cattleman* when London finally stepped out of her office.

"Any leads for new workers?"

"A few, we'll see what pans out."

I held open the front door and let London walk out. Bounding down the stairs, we each climbed onto a four wheeler and headed out to resume moving the water wheels.

London was in front, and when she got around the house, she screamed, and rolled the throttle on the ATV.

"I thought you said they were on timers." I raced after her.

"They are, we set them, you saw me."

When we reached a small outbuilding, what I could only assume was the pump house, London jumped off and headed toward the large copper knob. Moving around her, I grabbed one end and started turning until the cascade of water stopped. "When was the last time you checked them to make sure that they were working correctly?"

"Yesterday when Jack was using the wheels. He would have told me if there had been a problem."

But once we got to the irrigation systems, the hairs on the back of my neck were standing on end. I felt like someone was watching us, but I didn't see anyone else around.

"Fuck!" she shouted.

"What? We were only inside a few hours, how much damage could it cause?" I was showing my lack of ranch knowledge, but I'd seen rain last longer here.

"Jack and Ryan laid seed yesterday, and this much water more than likely tore up the top soil and washed all of that away. We are either going to have to wait a few weeks to see if anything starts to grow or reseed." Walking to the first irrigation system, London leaned down and examined the timer. "Motherfucker."

"Is it broken?"

"No. The timer was turned off, and the gallons per minute were turned up to the maximum. This was deliberate."

Yep, and I had a sinking suspicion who had done it. Unfortunately there was no sense trying to get fingerprints off it since it was farm equipment that they all had access to.

"We need to stop watering for the day. I need to give the soil time to absorb some of this water before I let the cattle out here."

I helped London roll up the hoses and pack up the water wheels, all the while trying to figure out how to approach her about the Ryan situation. I didn't believe for one second that she was with him, but if he thought they were together and was pissed that I was hanging around, well...

"Hey, so, I have to tell you something."

This earned me a suspicious smile, and I guessed I

deserved it. Saying that was the equivalent of telling your significant other that you needed to talk. It was the kiss of death.

"Go on."

"Yesterday when I got here, Ryan wasn't too happy to see me and told me that this was his farm and that you two were together."

"Are you freaking kidding me?"

"I wouldn't joke about something like that."

"No, he and I aren't together, and we have never been together. He has also never owned any part of this farm." London lifted the tongue of the water wheel's small trailer and hooked it onto the four wheeler's hitch.

"Why would he say that then?"

"I have no idea, but I'm at the end of my patience with him. I don't know what to do."

"I think that you're doing it by looking for new people. And until you replace him, you'll need to keep a closer eye on him whenever he's around."

"I'd already planned on that."

"Smart and beautiful."

I said it before I could think better of it, and the prettiest flush crept across her cheeks as she climbed onto the four wheeler.

I thought about the fire and how it wasn't the main pasture so it didn't debilitate the farm, just inconvenienced them. Same with the waterwheel, it didn't ruin the field just delayed it a day.

"Come on, cowboy, let's get this back to the house."

By the time we got everything unloaded and reached the stable, my sheriff instincts were on full alert. "Who are they?" I pointed to a woman standing with Ryan and one of the other guys who I had seen around here.

"That's Wally and his wife Ann." London started waving as we got closer. "Hi, Ann, how are you? I'm glad to see you."

"I'm great! I brought some fresh herbs over for Paris and was just talking to Wally and Ryan before heading home."

Her words were casual and light, but her expression seemed a little strained. I looked at Wally, who was fidgeting, and then to Ryan, who was smiling. That douche was up to something. I wasn't sure what, but I was going to find out.

7

LONDON

Having Braden around after the fire had been nice, but the last few days, he'd been working crazy hours and hadn't been around much. I was trying to get the ranch back to a normal—well, as normal as it could be with eighty fewer acres. Walking into the barn to get Mim, I froze at the sight of Wally and Ryan. Wally was oiling the saddles, but Ryan was posed as if ready to strike. His legs were spread shoulder-width apart, his hands rested on his hips, and his face was contorted like...mmm, well...he was constipated.

"Hello, Wally." His face brightened the moment he saw me.

"Hey, Ryan, you look uncomfortable. I think we have some castor oil that we use for the horses when they get clogged up if you need some." I was intending for my brevity to lighten the tension in the barn, but apparently it wasn't wanted. Both men's eyes narrowed. "What is y'alls problem? If you two are going to have a pissing match, I suggest that you do it when I'm not paying you. In other words, get over it and get to work." I scooted past them and opened Mim's stall.

When I glanced back, Wally was gone and Ryan was standing there staring at me. "Did you need something?"

"Yes, as a matter of fact, I do."

"Okay?"

"London, I have no clue what has gotten into you, but I don't like the way you are speaking to me. We are a team, and as such, you need to speak to me with respect."

Setting Mim's brush down, I gave Ryan my full attention. "Ryan, we are not a team. I am a team with my sisters. We are employee and employer. I will start speaking to you with respect once you regain some of my respect. You did not act this way when my father was around, and to be honest, I'm not sure how much longer I can continue having this conversation with you. If it wasn't for your years of service here, I'd already have terminated you for your attitude toward me."

"Let me tell you something, London, I stuck around all those years because I was the son your dad always wanted and never had."

Ryan's words pierced me. My dad had never said anything or acted as though he'd missed out on having a boy.

"Yeah, you think that he was all happy having three girls? Well, he wasn't. Why do you think he started the stables? He wanted to give you girls something since the ranch was no place for you. Horseback riding and Western riding lessons were more girl-friendly in his book. I was there for him to show the ropes to."

"Get out. Go home. Don't come back until you've adjusted your attitude." But Ryan didn't move. "Ryan, so help me god, if I have to tell you one more time, you will not have an opportunity to come back. I'd suggest that you go now."

Ryan strode out, but it took every ounce of my will power not to smack the ever-loving-shit out of him and knock that damn smirk off his face.

Once I knew he was gone, I pulled out my phone and sent my sisters a text.

ME: We need a Kelly meeting.

Paris: When?

Holland: How about now, where are you?

Me: Stables. Need to go for a ride and clear my mind.

Paris: On my way.

Holland: Me too.

MIM WAS MOVING AROUND, which made it ten times harder to get her saddle on, she was so in-tune with my emotions, and she could feel my tension.

"Where'd Ryan go?" Wally asked, looking around as he pulled his hat off. Beads of sweat lined his forehead, and he pulled a worn bandana from his back pocket to wipe them away.

"I sent him home." I led Mim out of her stall. "Wally, I don't know how much longer I can put up with his attitude. For some reason, he has the idea that he runs this place, and no matter how many times I correct him, he won't listen. I just don't want to put up with him."

"I'll have a talk with him. He's young."

"He's older than I am."

"Yeah, but you had your dad, and he was a great influence. Ryan hasn't had anyone since he was seventeen."

"He's had the influence of this family for the past fifteen

years. If he hasn't figured out how things are run by now, then maybe there's no hope for him."

"Oh, London, that's harsh. There's always hope."

"Can I ask you something?"

"Sure, kiddo, anything, you know that."

"Did my dad ever regret not having a boy?" Wally's face went blank, and I murmured, "I guess that is a yes."

"No, that isn't what that is. I'm pissed that you'd think that."

"Well, Ryan said I needed to treat him better since he was the son my dad always had wanted."

Wally shook his head. "Your dad wanted a son for one reason and one reason only, and that was to do the hard labor so he could try to force you girls to pamper yourselves more. But it wasn't because he actually wanted a son. Hell, once he saw your love for the ranch, he knew that everything was right as rain. That was why he built the stables."

"I'm not following you. What do the stables have to do with my love for the ranch? It only took away from our cattle land?"

"By the time you were sixteen, Samuel knew everything in his life was how it was supposed to be. He had great employees..."

"Or so he thought." I couldn't hold back my barb.

"You loved the ranch. Paris loved cooking and just being the little momma. And Holland was showing all signs of having a true love for horses. So your dad decided to build the stables for her; although, it belongs to all of you. But this way, each of you have your own domain to control. So, did he want a son? Sure, all guys want a son at first. Did he regret not having a son? Never once."

Placing one hand on Wally's shoulder, I leaned forward

and placed a kiss on his sun-weathered cheek. "Thanks. My sisters and I are going for a ride. I sent Ryan home and told him not to come back until he has a change of attitude. Maybe call Jack and ask him to come in this afternoon?"

"Will do. You three have fun."

I followed Wally's gaze to see my sister Paris's Jeep coming down the trail.

"Hey, you two. I got Ursula and Khan tacked up." They both darted off through the giant wooden doors, and several minutes later, the three of us were kicking up dirt at breakneck speeds across the pasture.

When we finally slowed to a trot, Paris pulled up next to me, asking, "So what's up?"

"It's Ryan. I sent him home today." I recounted this morning's events.

"You have to work with him more than we do, what's your gut telling you?" Paris's calm demeanor and rationale were a balm to my riled nerves.

"It's telling me that even after Wally talks to him, it won't get better."

"Then let's find someone else. Wally can help you until we hire a new ranch hand. I can handle the stables and lessons."

"That's a lot of work, Holland, are you sure?"

"Positive. It isn't as if I have anything else to do." She dismounted from her horse and wrapped his rein on a hook on the tree.

Paris and I followed suit.

"So, we're in agreement? The next time there is an issue with Ryan, he's gone regardless of the number of years he's been here?"

"Yep." Paris and Holland both nodded.

"Then do me a favor. Write down everything you can

think of—any instances you've seen of his insubordination —so we have them on file just in case we need them. I have a feeling he will give us trouble."

"You think?"

I busted up laughing, and then my smile fell slowly. "Ryan told me Dad always wanted a son, and he was that son." I watched my sisters' faces as my words sunk in. "He has a serious chip on his shoulder about something, so yes, I think he will cause us problems."

"What? You've got to be kidding me!" Holland shouted.

"I asked Wally about it, and he said that Dad never said such a thing. I think Ryan is just grabbing at straws to see how far he can push me."

"Sounds like it. So what did you say?"

"I sent him home."

"I'm tired of his crap. I think we should go ahead and fire him. I honestly doubt that his attitude will ever change. He has this hang up about women working, especially on a ranch," Paris said as she leaned back and made herself comfortable underneath a bushy palm tree.

"I'm on board. The guy is a dick. But we need to do this the right way," Holland warned. "He's become a real pig lately, and his thoughts about women being barefoot and pregnant—"

I interrupted Holland. "When did he say that?"

"He didn't, but he might as well have. You can tell by the way he says certain things. He just doesn't think we should be running this ranch. I hate his damn attitude. I mean, who the hell does he think he is? He isn't even related to us, and he thinks he's part of the family. He has nothing to do with the stables, but he's always there, introducing himself to the parents of my students. I love Daddy and all, but how the hell did he let a rat like that fool him?"

"Daddy didn't know how much of a prick Ryan was. You can't put that blame on him."

"I don't blame him. I just really miss him." Holland kicked at the sand under her feet.

"Barefoot and pregnant..." I thought aloud. "I could seriously see him saying just that."

We laughed, and it felt good, and a lot of the tension slipped away as we made our way back to the house.

When we broke the tree line, there was a black pickup truck sitting next to mine up at the house.

"I'll take care of Mim and Ursula, you two go on up." Holland held Mim's reins as I dismounted, then she moved and held the reins of Paris's horse while Paris dismounted. Holland headed to the stables while Paris trailed behind me as I dashed up to the house, excitement bubbling inside me.

I was excited to see Braden.

Shit.

I so needed to curb my excitement.

Coming up behind him, I admired his ass in tight jeans as he bent over and set a two-by-four into place to make one side of the frame for the garden bed. "Fancy seeing you here."

He quickly stood and turned to face me, a smile lighting his entire face. "I told you I'd be here."

"I know, but I wouldn't have blamed you had you not shown. You've done so much already, and it is your day off."

"Would it make you feel better if I took the night off..." Braden reached forward and swept a stray piece of hair out of my eyes, "with you?"

"What?"

"How about you and I go up to Marcus's for a beer when I'm done here?"

"Okay? But just for a beer, and as long as we both agree that it isn't a date."

"Fine, not a date. We can do something else if you want to."

"No, let's go. I'd like it. I need a night off."

The rest of the day flew by, but I didn't get much work done. Between watching Braden outside my office window and admiring the way the sweat trickled down his muscular, shirtless chest and Paris constantly going outside, Christ on a cracker, I was going to have a headache before I even stepped foot into the bar from all the loud slamming of our screen door. But I couldn't fault her excitement. I just hoped that she thanked Asher, who had worked just as hard as Braden had all day.

At eight o'clock, I was ready to relax. Braden had his arm around my waist, and I felt strangely possessive as we walked through the parking lot. I couldn't tell whether he was wearing cologne or if it was just his soap, but whatever it was, it smelled amazing.

The house band was playing some Brothers Osborne, and I loved the feeling of Braden's fingers as he picked up the tune and started strumming against my hip.

"Hey, you two, Yuenglings?" Marcus pulled two bottles up from under the counter and set them on top.

Braden reached in his pocket to pay, but Marcus refused our money.

"Give it up, he never lets me pay," I whispered into Braden's ear.

"Hey, Braden, have you ever heard this girl sing?"

"Umm no, can't say that I have."

"Yo, Derrick, can you play 'Fancy' by Reba?"

The guitarist turned around to his band then gave Marcus the thumbs-up.

"I hate you, Marcus. No. No."

"Oh, come on, London, I want to hear you." Braden gave me his cocky smile.

I glanced up and met Marcus's smirk as he signaled for the band to go ahead and start the beat. "Ugh." But when the first few notes trilled and the rhythm ran through me, I was five years old again, singing a song at the top of my lungs and having no clue what it meant.

I hopped up on the stage ready to give the crowd what they were cheering for and was handed the microphone. As I marched front and center, Braden's eyes followed me, which only made me give my performance a bit more jazz and my hips a little more wiggle.

When the song was over I had this strange feeling that something between me and Braden had shifted. I didn't know what to call it, him coming over, us hanging out, whatever. I did know that I was going to be forgiving him because I wanted a repeat of our one night.

As I stepped down from the stage, he handed me my beer, which I downed. A mixture of nerves and sweat from being center stage had a way of making a girl thirsty. When his strong hands removed the bottle and set it on the table next to me, he pulled me in tighter to his body.

"Dance with me."

I nodded. I didn't recognize the song at first, just the notes of a steel guitar but when the band joined in I recognized "Gonna Wanna Tonight" by Chase Rice.

I wondered if there was something prophetic that he was trying to say with the words of the song. But I shook my head. This man was a man whore, right? I mean, he'd left me with just a note. I couldn't be that mistaken about someone, could I? If this turned out to be one of his many moves he made to get women into the sack, I would geld him or I'd let Holland do it.

"You smell like strawberries." His warm breath played havoc on my body as it tickled the side of my neck.

"It's my shampoo."

"I wonder if you taste like strawberries too."

Before I could object, his mouth covered mine, and his tongue slipped between my lips. My tongue may not have responded, but my body had a mind of its own and was trying to meld into his on the fucking dance floor.

When the song ended, my mind was mush, except for one thought: *I'm kissing Braden fucking McManus.*

8

BRADEN

L eaving London at her front door was hard. I take that back, I was hard, leaving her was excruciating. But I'd fucked up our first night by leaving her. I'd overthought the situation instead of just letting it play out and seeing where it took us. I wasn't going to jeopardize the second chance she was giving me. When we took that step, I wasn't walking away again.

I had no clue how I was going to get through the next few days. I'd agreed to work some overtime since one of the guys was on vacation, and for the first time, I regretted that decision. Up until this point, I'd eaten, slept, and drank being a deputy, but London had me wanting to sneak away and spend time with her at the ranch.

It was after one in the morning when I pushed through my bedroom door. Grabbing the collar of my shirt, I yanked it up and over my head. The damn thing smelled like her and it made my dick hard. That particular problem, I ignored. Nothing but the real thing would alleviate the lust I had for that woman.

The next morning, the first call I had was a fatal car

wreck on State Road 46, and by the time traffic had
resumed, it was well after lunch. My next call brought me
out to Butterfly Lane. You'd think with a name like that it
would be peaceful, but if drugs, prostitution, or attacks on
law enforcement were going to happen, odds were it was
happening there.

When my shift ended, it was after midnight, but I still
found myself driving to see London. Her front porch lights
were illuminated, so I cut my lights and waited to see if
there was any movement inside, but there wasn't any.

Not really wanting to give up just yet, I waited. A few
minutes passed before a set of headlights cut through the
darkness and unease tightened my stomach. The new
vehicle pulled up to the side of the house. A tall figure
emerged from the driver's side, and from where I sat, it was
easy to tell it was a man, but it wasn't until he stepped into
the pool of light by the steps that I could tell who it
was—Ryan.

He strode to the front door and waited. It didn't take
long before London opened it, and it took even less time for
a weird sensation to work its way across my chest. I didn't
like the feeling at all. Holy shit, I was jealous. I was irritated
with myself for feeling that way. I knew London had
mentioned that Ryan was just another worker in the ranch–
a friend. He'd been working there for fifteen years for fuck's
sake, but it didn't take away this feeling.

Staying in my Explorer I fought the urge to go up there
since I didn't want London thinking that I was a stalker.
When Ryan leaned closer to London, I found myself
gripping the steering wheel tighter and calling all bets off. I
was going up. But before I could avert my gaze, she was
stepping back from him, her arms outstretched to ensure he
kept his distance. "That's my girl."

Shit, where had that come from?

It didn't matter. All that mattered was that Ryan has spun away from her and was walking back to his truck.

I tailed him, because...why wouldn't I?

The guy was slimy, and I was going to find out what he was up to, if for no other reason than to protect London and her sisters from that guy.

I followed him over to the next town, where he finally pulled up to some bar. I had never been here before, and obviously, I couldn't go in or he'd know that I had followed him. However, the Hitching Post was a dive if I ever saw one.

I called David, figuring he'd know something.

He answered on the first ring, "David here."

"Hey, it's me. Tell me what you know about the Hitching Post?"

"On 419?"

"Yep, that's the one."

"They're not the biggest fans of sheriffs. The owners are all right, but the manager is a real piece of work. Why?"

"I just followed that Ryan guy from the Kelly Ranch, I have a bad vibe about him."

"Why? He's just at a bar, nothing funny about that, maybe he lives around there."

"Nah, he lives in Geneva, I ran him after the fire."

"Stay where you are, I'm on my way." David disconnected.

I kept my eyes on the bar, but my mind wandered to London. I needed to convince her that actions spoke louder than words. Any guy could tell her that he adored her, but unless he showed it, the words truly meant nothing. I needed to show her what I was feeling and what I wanted.

Kind of made me think of Paris and Asher. That guy was

head over heels in love with her. I wondered why they weren't dating or hell, married.

I was still trying to work that one out when David walked up and knocked on my window.

Shit.

I rolled down the glass and met David's smirk. "Hey, is he still inside?"

"Yeah, his truck is right over there."

"No problem, I'm trusting your gut even if I'm not trusting your reasoning."

David went left, and I went right. We both walked around the bar, and except for the loud raucous noise and the smell of old sweat, nothing seemed out of the norm. The crowd looked rougher but that was to be expected, and through the side window I could see Ryan sitting at the bar.

"Do me a favor," I said to David when we met back at my SUV. "When you are on shift would you add the ranch onto your routine patrol?"

"Sure thing. This guy really bothers you, doesn't he?"

"Yeah, and I can't figure it out, which pisses me off all the more."

9

LONDON

I pulled on Mim's reins and scanned the grazing cattle. I'd been worried about Bovine Respiratory disease since it was brought on by stress, but Asher had just checked them out and told me they were all in good health. I was still glad I'd had them checked. I figured running from a blazing field had to be pretty stressful, and I couldn't be too careful.

At least something was going right.

Riding Mim over to a group of Sylvester palm trees, I got off her so that she could graze for a bit. Dad had planted the trees around the ranch since they were sturdy and required little maintenance, but his main intention was to offer a place for the ranch hands to have somewhere to rest, tie their horse, and eat. I could still see him and Wally sitting here eating their lunch. Sometimes they even brought the three of us and we'd join them.

"You look comfortable."

I shielded my eyes from the bright sun and saw Ryan standing there. I fought back my urge to groan.

"I'm headed out, anything else you need?"

"Since you came in today, I'm assuming you are ready to

work and respect me and my sisters as the owners and bosses of Kelly Ranch and Iron Horse Stables?"

Ryan's only answer was a chin nod.

Damn it. It wasn't the answer I wanted, but it would have to do for the moment.

He turned his gaze toward the burnt field. "Have they discovered anything yet?"

"Nope, not yet."

"Not to be rude, but maybe if the deputy would actually do his job instead of trying to win over Paris with the garden and you by helping with the pasture, maybe we would know something by now."

"Ryan, stop. You have no clue what you're talking about. I've known Braden since we were eleven. He's being kind and helping us, which is more than I can say about some people." I wasn't sure exactly what I was expecting, but it wasn't for Ryan to take a step toward me, his face twisted in impatience and a hint of anger.

He opened his mouth to say something else, but the sound of approaching hoof falls stopped him, and we both turned toward the sound.

"Holy shit, he's riding Jafar." Not positive as to which was sexier—the stallion that was still somewhat wild or the man riding against the setting sun with suntanned skin, black hair, and a hint of danger to him. No, it wasn't that he was dangerous in a physical sense. He was dangerous to my sanity and possibly to my heart.

I turned back to Ryan. "Why don't you go on home? We still have a lot to do around here, and tomorrow will be another tiring day." When Ryan didn't say anything or move to heed my word, I continued. "I think that it's best that you leave now."

Ryan turned and headed back toward the horse he'd ridden over on.

"What was that about?" Braden asked as he tied Jafar's reins around a tree.

"Nothing." I watched him as he confidently moved around the horse. "When did you learn to ride?"

"I grew up around here, did you forget that?"

"No, just didn't picture you as an equestrian."

"Well, I'm probably not as skilled as you are, but I know enough not to get killed. Maybe we can race some time and see who would win."

I let out a laugh. I'd been riding since I was three, roping since I was five, and jumping since I was ten. Yeah, it wouldn't be fair, but I wouldn't tell him all that. "Sure, why not."

"Now, are you going to tell me what Ryan wanted and why he looked so mad when I showed up?"

"He was being typical Ryan."

"Giving you trouble?" Braden looked truly concerned as he slowly moved toward me.

"Nothing more than usual. I just really need to hire someone though."

Braden stared at me as if carefully considering his words. "I can help on my days off."

"Thanks, but I can't ask you to do that. If you could keep your ears open about anyone looking for a job, I would appreciate it."

Braden stepped forward and pulled me against him before placing a gentle kiss on the tip of my nose. "Okay." He tucked a strand of hair that covered my face behind my ear. That was not the first time he did such a thing. It seemed extremely intimate, and I liked it.

"What are you doing here?"

"I just got off, so I thought that I'd stop by and see you. Holland told me to head out to the pasture."

"But Jafar, I'm shocked that he'd let you ride him. He generally only lets Holland ride him."

"I don't know what to tell you. Holland made me hold out my hands and walk from horse to horse. She said that she was judging how they responded to my scent."

"Yeah, she reads a lot of Native American books on how they lived 'one with the land and animals.'"

"I guess that Jafar chose me. He seems like a good horse, a lot of energy though."

I let out a laugh at his response. "Yeah, he's a wild one." Meeting Braden's eyes was a huge mistake, they were too bright, and he was too handsome. Yep, Braden was very dangerous.

"Let's head back." I looked toward the sun to keep my gaze off him and decided I'd been out riding for too long, and Mim had to be getting thirsty. Mounting my horse, I turned my focus to him. With Mim's reins held tight, I got into position. A devilish idea played in the corner of my mind; if he agreed, I'd dash off like lightning.

"Care to make a friendly wager?" I winked, daring him to say no.

"Sure, what's the bet and what are the stakes?"

"A race back to the stables."

"What does the winner get?" He lifted one brow, and god, that gesture made me squirm. "How about the loser has to grant the winner three wishes?"

"Huh?" Oh shit, that was some serious stuff, and I wasn't sure if I wanted to win the wishes or lose just to see what he would come up with.

Decisions, decisions.

"Not so confident now, are you? You afraid you might lose?"

Braden's taunting words hit their mark. "Fine." I was going to destroy him. "First one to hit the dirt drive."

"Deal. Are you ready?" Braden gave me a wink."

I couldn't believe that I had just agreed to race Braden fucking McManus, and if he won, he could ask me to do anything...as in *anything*.

He cleared his throat. "On your mark, get set, go."

I dug my heels into Mim's sides, and she was off. Lowering my body toward the crest, I grinned and knew she was happy that I was allowing her full reign.

I glanced back, needing to see where Braden was, and almost fell. He was right beside me. I squeezed Mim's sides a little more to spur her on, but Braden did the same thing and was already pulling up next to me.

"Shit. Come on, Mim. Don't let those boys win." I heard Braden's deep, throaty laugh as my words carried to him, but they only spurred him on.

"You're going to regret this, McManus." But Braden was so far ahead he probably couldn't hear me over the thundering of hooves.

"Come on, Mim. We can't lose this one!" Keeping up with Braden and Jafar had been harder than I thought. Jafar was a faster horse, but I was a better rider. My ego wouldn't allow me to believe anything different.

Mim raised her front legs and switched from a run to a canter, high-stepping as she fought me to turn away from the barn

"Whoa, Mim, what spooked you?" I leaned forward and patted her. "Calm down, girl." I turned at the sound of Braden, who was trying to calm Jafar. "Something isn't right. Let's go." Lightly kicking my heels into Mim, I encouraged her to pick up her pace, and as she neared the stables, I heard it.

"Something's wrong."

"Slow down, London, don't go running in there," Braden ordered.

"Don't be silly, you were just in there a little while ago. It's the horses, something's wrong."

"I understand that, but I also know that we haven't caught whoever charred eighty acres of your ranch either. You and I were out there at least an hour, that's plenty of time, now stay back."

As his words sank in, I did as he'd ordered and slowed my pace. Sliding off Mim, I sent her out to the paddock with Jafar.

Bending down, Braden pulled out a 9mm from his boot holster and held it down to his side. With his left arm, he held me back, urging me to go slowly. Our steps were soft as we moved forward, but the only sounds were from the horses and they were full of pain.

The first stall was Shere Khan's, and my heart hurt for him because he was on his side, sweat dripping down his forehead and sides.

Before I took another step, I called Holland.

"Hello? London? Are you okay?"

Tears were streaming down my face. "Call Asher and wake up Paris. I need you both down at the stables immediately."

"Tell me what's wrong?" Fear laced Holland's words.

"I don't know what's wrong, just hurry." I disconnected and then stepped away from Khan to examine the rest of the horses.

"The stables are clear," Braden hollered from the other end.

I nodded as I moved to Ursula, who was thrashing back and forth, her stomach making a loud rumbling sound. In the stalls behind me, Gaston and Tremaine were equally as sick. I worked my way down, each one of them was sick...every one except Jafar and Mim, who had been out with us.

"When do the horses get their last feed?" Braden was in full deputy mode.

"At four o'clock." I looked at the screen on my phone. "That was almost three hours ago."

"So, Jafar and Mim had eaten before I arrived, correct?"

"Yeah."

"Then it wasn't their food."

The high beams from the truck lights were aimed right into the open stable doors, then Holland jumped out as she ran to Shere Khan. Paris moved to Ursula and fumbled to get the gate open. "Asher is on his way."

"What happened?" Holland asked again.

"I don't know. Braden and I were out and when we got back, Mim and Jafar started acting weird, like they sensed something. When I got close, I heard them, they were all whinnying. But it can't be something they ate because Mim and Jafar are fine."

"I'd say that it was colic, you know? The rolling over, the sweating, but there is no way they all have colic at the same time." Holland was bending over to rip off first one boot and then the other. Apparently, in her haste to get out of the house, she'd put them on the wrong feet. At any other moment, that would have been funny.

"It has to be Asher," Paris said as tires sped over gravel.

It was, and the second he jumped from the truck, he grabbed a large duffle bag and started barking questions, "What else, besides rolling? What other symptoms?"

"Sweating and elevated heart rate," Holland shouted as she moved to him.

He nodded. "Marcus is coming behind me. I didn't want to waste time hooking up my veterinary trailer, so he's bringing it with the rest of my equipment and medicine we might need." Asher stepped into the first stall to get a better look.

My heart broke at the look of desperation in the horse's eyes. They had no clue what to do. "It's going to be okay, girl, Asher's going to make you better, I promise." I moved next to Yzma, a foal from early this year that had just been weaned. She was still so small that a churning fear took root in my stomach.

"What the fuck?" I looked up to see Marcus strolling into the barn.

"Hey, Braden, I need you and Marcus to start helping the girls clear out all of the hay from the stalls."

"Got it." Braden moved to a wall and picked up a rake.

"London, I need you to call Wally and the others and get them in here now." I pulled out my phone and started dialing.

"Holland, I need you to start giving each of the horses some activated charcoal to keep any more poison for absorbing into their system."

"Poison?" we all asked in unison.

"Yes, I'm not sure which plant, but from the symptoms I'd say it was a hemlock variety or oleander. Paris and I will start administering the anti-arrhythmic drugs." Then he turned to Paris and cupped her cheeks in his palms to make sure she was paying attention. "I need you to go check their heart rate and get a base idea of temperature. I'm going to start with Yzma, but let me know who appears to be in the worst shape so I can move to them next. Can you do that?"

A tearful Paris nodded. "Got it," was all she said before moving to the end of the barn to start with the first stall.

As I waited for the first call I had to make to connect, I stared at the horses, blaming myself for what had happened. If I hadn't been out riding, flirting with Braden, or whatever, I would have been here. I would have been doing my damn job, running the ranch, and then maybe I would have noticed something or someone. Wally's voicemail picked up, and I left him a quick message, telling him to get to the stables as soon as he could and then hung up. I got ahold of both Jack and Ryan, and both assured me they were on their way.

"I don't get it, who could do something like this?" Holland heard me ask as I slipped my phone into my pocket and looked around the barn, feeling as lost as I probably looked. Holland moved from stall to stall, squirting liquid activated charcoal into each horse's mouth. "An animal, and not the sweet, gentle kind like a horse."

I couldn't have said it better myself.

I worked with Braden and Marcus, raking, shoveling, and piling any possibly contaminated hay into a giant pile away from the horses. We were halfway done when someone appeared at my side. "What can I do to help?" I turned to see Wally.

"Help Marcus and Braden start clearing out the stalls of any leftover hay. We need to destroy it."

"On it. I'll pull a tractor around and we can load it up on there." Wally headed out.

I joined Holland and helped her with the charcoal, and when we were done, we started clearing out the tack and water pails that we kept in each stall.

An icy chill tore through me at the sound of Paris's sobs, and I dropped the buckets and raced to where I had heard her. She was in Yzma's stall, the foal's little head was lying peacefully in her lap. Paris pulled her fingers through the tousled creamy mane that was splayed out.

My eyes filled with tears as I dropped to my knees next to her and took in the sight before me. I didn't have to ask what was wrong. I could see it for myself. There was no rise and fall to the gentle horse's chest and no soulful look in her dark eyes.

"Honey, Yzma was too small, she couldn't fight it."

"She shouldn't have had to. Whoever did this murdered her. She should have been safe here." Paris half-cried, half-shouted.

"I know, and I promise we will find out who is doing this."

"Ursula is going to be so sad. This was her baby, her first baby." Paris continued brushing her fingers through the horse's mane as she rocked back and forth.

I held Paris until her sobs quieted, but I didn't try to make her get up when I stood. I just backed quietly out of the stall and went in search of Asher.

"How is she?" he asked, and the anguish on Asher's face was almost as heart-rending as it had been on Paris, but I think his pain was for an entirely different reason. Yes, Asher hated losing an animal, but I knew he hated not being Paris's rescuer even more.

"She's hurt and angry at whoever did this. She just needs some time alone. What can I do to help you?"

"I need you to start working on getting each stall sterilized. Start with the empty four, and then we will move some of the horses there as soon as we can get them standing or onto a cot. Then we will clean the other ones as we get them vacated. Leave Yzma until the end."

I did as he asked, and by the time the stalls were deemed

daft, we'd worked through the night and morning and it was already two in the afternoon. Ryan, Jack, and Wally had buried Yzma, and Paris was inside quiet and sad.

"We are going to need to watch them, the next seventy-two hours will be vital," Asher said as he gathered his supplies.

"Their symptoms? Are they normal reactions? I mean, does that happen the first time a horse is exposed or after a long period of exposure to the poison?" Braden stood next to me. He was asking questions that I should be asking, but truth was, I hadn't thought of them.

"The symptoms are normal when ingesting the poison. I'd say the poison was in their system all of a few hours. I'm going to send some fecal matter off to be tested and know for sure which poison was used. But like I said, the next several hours you'll need to watch them around the clock."

"London and I will take first watch." Braden wove his fingers in-between mine.

Swallowing hard, I gave him a faint smile as hopelessness started to wash over me. I hated it, but part of this was my fault. No, I would never do anything to hurt the horses, but the ranch and stables were partially mine to take care of, and in less than a month, we'd had a massive fire, a minor flood, and almost every one of our horses had been poisoned.

"London, I only have one lesson today, but I forgot to cancel her with all this chaos. Is it okay if I use Mim?" Holland grabbed a child-sized saddle and turned to look at me.

"Of course, you know that you never have to ask. I trust you." I waved her on. "Ryan and Jack, if you two could go herd the cattle to the small pasture and make sure they are okay, you can head home after." After the two men were out of earshot, I turned to Wally. "I need you to step up and assume the leadership role of the three of you. I've been looking for a new field hand, but I need you to know that I plan to let Ryan go, which means you are going to be in charge. He reports to you, not me."

I caught hold of Braden's eyes and could tell that he'd prefer I just get rid of Ryan, but after tonight, I needed all the help that I could get.

"Is something wrong?" Wally looked anything but pleased by my decision.

"Honestly? Yes, I don't appreciate the way he treats me. My sisters aren't too fond of him either."

"What if I talk to him?"

"You can talk to him and tell him to cool it if he wants to keep his job, but as far as being in charge, that is me and my sisters, and he still reports to you."

Wally didn't say another word as he headed toward the barn doors.

"I need to get to the bar, Jett will need some help." Marcus stepped up to me and gave me a kiss on my cheek. "Call if you need anything or learn of anything." I leaned into Marcus and soaked in his strength, the familiarity that was like a big brother.

"I need to file a report and get an investigation going on this."

I hadn't even thought about pressing charges or police reports. "This is such a mess, all of it, first the fire, then the pasture being soaked, now this."

"Look at me." I met his eyes. "I will figure this out, promise. Aside from the three of you who else goes in and out of the barn?" Braden settled on top of an old chest in one corner where we stored saddle blankets.

"Wally, Jack, and Ryan. But Asher and Marcus come and

go as they please." I turned to face my sister when she let out a loud *humph*. Holland raised an eyebrow as if casting judgment on me for even mentioning their names. "I'm not accusing Marcus or Asher, and Braden knows that. He asked who else has access. We also have a farrier who comes by twice a month, but he was here last week."

"What do you know about Jack?" Braden had his phone open and was entering information as I spoke.

"He's been working here about twenty years. Was married, wife died a few years ago, no kids. He'd spend all his time here if we'd let him. There's no way he'd do something as horrible as this."

"Besides that, he mainly works with the cattle."

Shoving all the bad ideas aside, I chanted in my head that I needed to trust our workers. I had to believe in them because if I didn't, I might as well fire them all.

"Whoever did this wants to see the ranch hit rock bottom." Holland's voice was grim. She was staring at her horse, Shere Khan, who was starting to look a little better.

"You guys should be on the watch out. I really think the person who poisoned the horses is the one responsible for the fire and probably the flooded field. I know that had no permanent damage, so you didn't take it seriously, but at this point, I wouldn't rule out any sort of mishap." Braden made sure that Holland and I were both paying attention before he continued. "This can't be entirely coincidental. I have been thinking about this a lot lately, especially since I haven't gotten any new details on the arson case. Cases like this oftentimes end up being an inside job."

"What? Why would you think that?"

"I bet it is our neighbor," Holland scoffed. "He's mad that he isn't making money off us. He'd thought he'd force our hand by flooding the pasture and now this."

"You think?" I looked at Braden for answers.

"I'll talk with him, and I'll mention it to the fire investigator but truthfully I doubt it was your neighbor. More than likely it was one of the three guys that just left here. Whoever did this knew your schedule. They knew when the cattle were in which area and when you all locked up for the night."

I turned to Holland, my gut telling me that Braden was only half-right. I agreed that it wasn't our cranky neighbor, mainly because I doubted the guy who breeds horses would be as heartless as to poison them for some petty revenge, but our employees? I just couldn't fathom it.

"How could you doubt our guys, though? Why would they try ruining their livelihood? That doesn't make sense. Ruining us would ruin them."

"Unless ruining your ranch proves that you need them. London, can't you think of anyone who wants to prove that you are incapable of running the ranch? Someone who—"

"I get it, you are hinting to Ryan. Yes, he is an ass, but I don't think he'd ruin our ranch. I just think he is a chauvinistic pig."

"Don't rule it out, ruining us could force us to sell dirt cheap and give an asshole neighbor the opportunity to buy our land for a steal." Holland wasn't letting the idea of the neighbor go.

"Listen, I'm not ruling anyone out, we shouldn't be too quick to accuse anyone just yet. But at the same time, don't let your guard down." Braden reached over and squeezed my hand.

Shaking my head, I stood and shot him and Holland an angry look. "I can't believe that this was done by someone we think of as family. But I do believe that the person who poisoned the horses was also the one who set the fire."

With that, everyone nodded. At least we all agreed on one thing. I began pacing but stopped and looked up when I heard the stable doors opening, Ryan had entered the barn.

"We're having a private discussion," I said, not wanting Ryan lurking around or making comments about how this proved females couldn't handle the ranch.

"Private?" Ryan raised one eyebrow as he and Braden locked eyes in a death stare.

Braden squared his shoulders before speaking, his voice the most authoritative I'd ever heard. "If you have any idea who might want to do this to the girls, you should tell me now. The fire may not be something that I can investigate because it isn't my area, but this is something I can, and will, pursue. So, that means I will dig deep, and when I find the person responsible, I will find every charge I possibly can and throw it at them."

Ryan simply shrugged. "I have no clue. Well, Wally told me to come in and make sure the horses all had full water buckets. So that's what I'm going to do, if you all will excuse me." He stalked toward the first stall door, not looking back at us.

"Ryan, I'm taking care of the horses right now. Besides I told you to go on home. If you want to help then that is fine, but you can go on and help Wally with something else. Tell him that we've got this part handled."

Ryan stomped toward the barn doors, clearly not happy about being ordered around.

"Well, whoever did this has royally fucked up, my hands were somewhat tied with the fire. But this? This is my department. I'm going to give it everything I have," Braden said a bit too loud, obviously intending Ryan to hear him before he was out of hearing range. "I don't care what it takes, I'll be here day and night, I promise."

Day and night? Did Braden just insinuate that he'd be sleeping here? What. The. Heck? On one hand, it was comforting knowing that we'd have the extra protection, but on the other hand, I needed to refocus and pay attention to the ranch before I lost everything Daddy had ever worked for. But then again, the thought of a replay of our one night seemed to make my girly parts happy.

Braden glanced at me, and from the look on his face, I could tell he knew I wasn't listening to whatever he was saying. Heat rose on my cheeks, and his lips lifted in a half smile as if he knew what I'd been thinking.

"What?" I snapped.

"Nothing, I just like looking at you. How you holding up?"

"I've been better." I stepped away from him. "I...I'm just wondering what do we do next? Do we constantly sleep with one eye open until this gets solved, do Paris, Holland, and I need to come up with a rotation so that one of us is always on watch duty, what?"

"Sweetheart, let's get some rest, we will worry about all of that in the morning. We are going to solve this, I promise. I told you, I'm going to figure this out. Tonight, our focus is on the horses and just watching them and making sure they are okay." Braden pulled me into his arms and then covered my lips with his. I moaned and found myself lost in one of his addicting kisses, lost from the world of chaos going on around us. Yep, every ounce of will I had just went out the window, I wanted this man. One-night stand, stupid note, and all. He was a fabulous kisser and right then, he made me feel incredibly safe.

10

BRADEN

I waited on the front porch as London ran inside to grab a few things, and while she did, I put in a call to David.

"Hey, Lieutenant," David greeted on the other end of the phone.

"You won't believe the shit storm going on at the Kelly Ranch now. Someone poisoned the horses, and one of the foals died. I've done a sweep of the property, and everything else seems to be okay, but I need two favors."

"Sure, you name it."

"I need you to run down to technical services and checkout a few fingerprinting kits. I'll call ahead and give them a heads-up that you'll be picking them up."

"You got it. You think someone left something behind?"

"Even if they had, there were so many people in and out that whatever was there is useless. I want them just in case something else happens."

"I take it you won't be in tonight?"

"Nope, which brings me to my second favor. I need to you to run them down here for me."

"I'm on it. See you in thirty." David disconnected, and I slid my phone into my pocket.

"What's he bringing over?"

I turned to find Holland standing at the bottom of the steps. I hadn't realized she was there, let alone listening to my conversation.

"He's grabbing me some fingerprinting equipment in case anything else happens."

She nodded and blew out a deep breath. "Smart idea."

"You really think it's the neighbor?"

"Truthfully? No. He just gets me so angry that I want to blame everything that goes wrong in the world on him. But no, I don't think it's him."

"Then who do you think wants to hurt your family?"

Holland gave me a wry smile. "Ryan Cardenas. I don't trust that bastard."

"Mind telling me why him?"

Holland eyed me. "You might think this is stupid. But it's because no animals around here really like him. When he tries riding Jafar, Jafar runs and bucks until Ryan finally calls it and gets off. The same thing happens with Dad's stallion, Balthazar. Balthazar is the kindest among all the horses around. Anyone but Ryan can ride him. There is just something about the whole scenario that rubs me the wrong way." Holland and I leaned on against the split rail banister of the porch and looked out toward the three-quarter moon.

I knew that animals were good judges of character. Hell, we saw it with the K-9 units all the time.

"Cujo hates him too."

"Who's Cujo?"

"Asher's dog, he's a Golden Retriever."

"A Golden Retriever named Cujo seems like sort of an oxymoron."

"Asher had to stop bringing him after he tried to attack Ryan. It's always bothered me since the only person that Cujo protects more than Asher is Paris. I still swear that Ryan was doing something that Cujo believed was going to hurt Paris because Asher wasn't around and no one had ever seen the dog react that way before." Holland finished explaining her thought process about Ryan.

The more I heard about Ryan the more I seriously disliked the guy and the more I hated that London hadn't just fired him.

London appeared in the doorway and then made her way over to Holland and me.

"Yeah, the dog is the sweetest." London had obviously overheard part of our conversation.

"You ready to get back to the stable?" I asked as I slid the bag from her shoulder and draped my arm over her shoulders.

"Yeah, I think I got everything we might need." She smiled at me before turning to her sister. "I'll call you if any of them look like they are taking a turn for the worse. Don't worry."

I pressed a kiss to her temple as I helped her into my truck and we made our way back to the stables. When we got there, Balthazar was resting his head on the door of the stall and it was as if a weight started to lift from my chest. The horses weren't out of danger yet, but Balthazar looked to be on the mend. London grabbed a pail of fresh oats and hay with some enzymes that Asher had mixed up for us to start feeding them.

When the stallion took pieces of the straw, London's face brightened.

"He's eating, that's a good sign." Her voice echoed across the barn. "We'll just need to make sure that they stay hydrated, that's imperative."

I nodded to let her know that I understood as I moved to grab a few water pails. When we were finished refreshing the water and seeing which horses would eat a little, London and I made our way to where several bales of hay were stacked.

"You want to sit in the back room where there's a table or do you want me to grab some blankets and just stay out here with the horses?"

I caressed her cheeks with my thumbs as I cupped her face. "We can stay out here, it would probably make you feel better."

"You wouldn't mind camping on blankets?"

"Of course not." I was pretty sure that if I told her I would sleep on sharp rocks if it made her happy, she would freak out, so I just smiled and straightened the blankets that had been piled on the hay.

"David will be here in a little bit, he's bringing me something."

"Yeah? What is he bringing?"

"Just some fingerprint kits in case I need them."

"Can I play with the black powder you guys use?"

"I'll let you play with the black powder if you can keep me entertained."

"Don't go there, McManus."

I winked at her. "What, I didn't mean anything bad. Is it my fault if you took it there? I was thinking that you could come up with another one of your famous games. I could always use three more wishes."

"Okay, we'll play a game." She eyed me skeptically and

then grinned. "I guess it's only fair since we didn't get to finish our last challenge."

"Bullshit, I won, and you know it. I get those first three wishes."

She was staring at me through her long, dark lashes, it was so feminine and so unlike London that I doubted she knew she was doing it. "If I catch you staring at me like that again, I'll definitely think you're crushing on me."

She rolled her eyes. "As if. Excuse me, McManus. I'm not one of those girls who is going to fawn all over you."

"Good for you. I've never liked those kinds of girls. So, about my three wishes..."

"Okay. Just remember that this isn't *Fear Factor*, nothing gross, okay?"

"Don't worry, I'm not going to make you do anything like that," I reassured her. "My three wishes are all going to be used on dates. Three wishes; three dates."

Her eyes widened as if she couldn't believe that I'd ask something so innocent. "That's it?"

"That's it. That's all I'm asking for." I held my hands up in surrender.

"These were wishes without any sort of restrictions, and you're using them for dates?"

"I am. I liked the other night when we went to the bar. I want us to spend some more time together, just the two of us."

"You could have just asked me out."

"I could have, but then you could have said no again. Plus, now I have a chance to prove to you that I'm not the man whore you think I am and that one night we spent together wasn't something I actually do very often."

"You're not joking, are you?"

I shook my head.

"Okay, three dates. Just give me a heads-up so I can get ready in time since I'm always so yucky after working on the ranch all day."

"Fine. But are we still playing another game for wishes? I could always use three more. I might not be so innocent next time."

"No wishes." She laughed. "It's just a good way to pass the time and keep you entertained, as you so requested."

"Okay. So, what is the game?"

"Two truths and one lie. I'm going to say three things, and you have to guess which one is the lie." London's eyes twinkled with excitement. I couldn't help but smile knowing that she was concocting some astronomical tales.

"Okay. Let me go first." London nodded, allowing me first chance. "I've never tried bungee jumping. I don't drink soft drinks. I don't like kiwi."

She smirked. "Easy. You don't drink soft drinks."

I made a buzzing sound, and London gasped in surprise. "No way I'm wrong."

"I don't like kiwi."

She frowned. "That's a crime, they're delicious!"

"Nope. They are also gross. Your turn."

London licked her lips, making my muscles tense. I was even more amazed how much self-control I could muster not to jump her right here.

London clenched her right hand into a fist and released her pinky finger. "I drive tractors."

I smirked. That was obvious.

"I can't cook." She released another finger. "I like cats."

Shaking my head, I couldn't help but smile. I already knew that London couldn't cook, which was why I figured the first date would be at my house, but I didn't want to ruin her fun.

"Easy. You don't like cats."

She puckered up her lips into a cute pout.

"I'm wrong?"

"Yep. I love cats, but I hate Siamese cats. I tried to adopt one back in high school because I thought they were really cute. You know, *Lady and the Tramp*, we are Siamese. But it refused to listen to me. The bitch kept scratching my face and pissing on my bed. I finally had to get rid of her because Dad said that he was going to throw her into a combine even though we didn't have one. But I still like cats in general." She rolled her eyes. God, she looked beautiful when she did that. Okay, she looked beautiful no matter what she did. "We're tied, one point each."

"I thought you said that we weren't keeping score?" I raised one brow.

"No, I said no bets. I didn't say anything about not keeping score. Let's talk about high school. You went first for round one, so I'll go first for round two."

For a moment there, I thought about pulling London close and kissing her savagely and repeating our first night together, but I decided that I better take it slow and settled for watching her lips. The way her mouth opened and how she occasionally stuck the tip of her tongue out to moisten her lips was almost hypnotic.

"All right. I like biology. I joined the drama club. I got into a fight with Jenny Owens."

I furrowed my brows. Jenny Owens had been the head cheerleader at Oviedo High School. Why would London get into a fight with her?

"Okay, this is a tough call. You did a bang-up Reba act, but back in high school you seemed so much more shy and quiet, not to mention drama club was always full of the Emo kids, which you definitely aren't. But I don't see you as loving biology, maybe agriculture, but not bio. God, and I can't see you getting into a fight either. I'm stumped on this one." I rubbed my chin and watched her face for any sign of which one might be the lie.

"Just guess, there are no prizes, remember?" London taunted.

"Fine, I choose the third one. The lie is, you got into a fight with Jenny."

London winced. "Wrong. I did not join the drama club. And yes, I got into a fight with Jenny Owens."

"What? You really did? Why? How come I never heard about this? Jenny and I—"

"Dated, forever." London rolled her eyes while finishing my sentence.

"Yep, she thought I was trying to get her boyfriend's attention. You should have seen her, she burst onto the field at an Equestrian Club meet and started screaming about how I was trying to steal her guy."

I paused and tried to put the pieces together. Jenny had been a bitch but had never come across as the jealous sort. If anything, she tried to make me jealous.

"I can tell that you don't believe me." London extended her legs and crossed her ankles. "I knew you wouldn't have the slightest idea about this. Jenny was just a plain bitch, after all. I told her to take her bitching somewhere else. Then proceeded to have Grim kick dirt on her."

"Feisty. I must have been living under a rock back in those days. That would have been huge talk on the campus."

"It was. But I guess you guys were busy taking one too many blows to the head during football games. Never thought y'all would come out with your brains intact."

I leaned forward until our faces were an inch apart. I crooked a finger under her chin and lifted her head a little so that our eyes could lock and our noses touched. "So, you still think that I don't have a brain?"

London blushed, which made my cock twitch. I was fucking falling for this woman.

"It's debatable." She lightly punched my arm. "It's your turn. Tell me something about high school."

"Right. Okay. I was on the football team…"

London snorted and then rolled her eyes, obviously bored.

"I'm a man whore…"

I knew that she'd think this was easy.

"I had a crush on you in high school."

Confusion hit her first and then surprise before she finally settled on embarrassment. I waited for her to say something as she fiddled with her fingernails. "You had a crush on me."

"Yup, I've had a crush on you since maybe, like, sixth grade?"

"No, you didn't." London's face was masked in disbelief.

"Yep, all I know is that you used to smile at me when you passed me in the hallways and it was the best part of my day. Then when we were in high school, it seemed as if every year I had to work harder and harder to make you smile. Then you just stopped. You wouldn't even look at me anymore. I always wondered what I did wrong."

"I remember, that was the same year that I got into a fight with Jenny."

"And as far as my being a man whore. I really wish you'd stop saying that. I'm not that guy you've concocted in your mind and I'm not sure why you think that about me. I've been with you nonstop for a few weeks, have I done anything to perpetrate that belief?"

"Well…no."

"Then will you let it rest? We've been out of school for twelve years, and now we're here." I tightened my grasp on her hand and brought it closer to my mouth, planting a kiss on her knuckles. "I'm glad we've reconnected, maybe this is our chance that we never got."

She tilted her head and rested her cheek against my fingers.

I loved sitting here with her and hated when David showed up, but if I had any hope of figuring out who was creating havoc around here, I had to get to work.

BRADEN

"Hey, you two," Holland whispered as she pulled open the barn door. "I'm on watch now plus Wally, Jack, and Ryan just got here, so why don't you go on into the house."

London stood, stretched, and then tried to stifle a yawn. "Okay, horses appear to be doing better, so I think we are out of the scary zone for the most part."

"Got it. If anything changes, I'll come find you. Now, go get some real sleep in a real bed instead of on the floor of the barn."

London nodded, and I followed her up the path toward the house, only when she pulled the front door open, I didn't move to follow her inside.

"I'm going to head home, but what do you think about coming by my house tonight?"

"You mean like a date, as in our first date?"

"Yep, date one. We won't stay out late. I'll pick you up around six?"

"I can drive since you won the race, I should make a bigger effort." London squeezed my hand.

"Okay, see you tonight." I smiled and let her fingers drift from mine as she backed away and into the house. When I turned toward my truck, Ryan was there.

"Lieutenant McManus, do you ever go home?"

Ryan extended a hand and I obliged. His grip was tight, and I returned the favor with a smirk playing on my mouth. There was no point in trying to hide my dislike of this man since the feeling was reciprocated.

"Actually, yes, Mr. Cardenas, I'm heading home right now. You see, London and I have a date tonight." Ryan's jaw twitched in anger.

That's right, asshole, get mad, get real mad, and maybe you'll fuck up just enough that I can catch your ass.

But Ryan's demeanor changed when he noticed something behind me. I shifted and then glanced over my shoulder to find Wally making his way in our direction.

"How's the investigation going with the fire?" He widened his stance—a typical bully move to make himself appear bigger.

"Actually, I don't know. You see, a fire investigator handles that, and then they give us their final report. So, until they've crossed all their T's and dotted their I's, I'm just hanging back, biding my time, while they gather all the evidence to hang the son-of-a-bitch who did it."

"Well, since this isn't even your case, exactly why are you here all the time? We are a working ranch, not a playground." Disdain laced every single word he practically spit.

"It isn't my job, but my interest. I want to make sure the girls are safe."

Ryan laughed dryly, putting a hand on my left shoulder, which only made me want to swing on him.

"I must warn you, Braden, don't try to get your hands on

something that doesn't belong to you. Leave the girls alone, especially London. She's off limits."

I narrowed my gaze and pushed his grip off me. "Interesting that she seems to have a different opinion. According to her, she's single. Plus, she and I have known each other since we were kids, Mr. Cardenas. There's nothing wrong with me trying to console a friend, right?"

Ryan scoffed, blowing a puff of air on my face. "You're taking advantage of someone who is emotionally unstable."

I laughed. "She isn't emotionally unstable. She's having a rough time because of the bullshit going on around here. And I am willing to help." I patted his shoulder, making sure I'd put enough pressure on each blow before I pulled open my truck's door.

"By the way, Mr. Cardenas, you might want to tread very carefully. The next time you try to corner me and warn me away, I might not be in such a good mood. And...I might consider it harassment or intimidation on a law enforcement officer." I slammed my door before he said anything else.

WHEN MY DOORBELL RANG, I had to tell myself to be cool. Then, when I actually opened the door and saw London standing there, I had to tell myself again. She wasn't wearing her typical jeans. No, she was wearing a cream-colored dress that rested above her knees and a pair of bright-red cowboy boots. Her blonde hair was down, and all I wanted to do was sink my hands into it and pull her closer to me. And her eyes, with her hair down framing her face, reminded me of a glass of whiskey.

"You are breathtaking. Come in." I reached out a hand and escorted her in. "Can I fix you a drink?"

"Sure, what do you have?"

"Water, tea, beer, and wine."

"How about iced tea for now?"

"You got it. So after I left, did Ryan do anything or did any shit happen around the ranch?"

"No, why?"

"After you went inside, he decided to take it upon himself to warn me away from you."

"Oh, for fuck's sake! Are you kidding me?"

"Nope." I handed London her glass of tea. "He seems to be very territorial where you're concerned. He wanted me to know that the two of you have been together since you were fifteen and the ranch was pretty much his."

"That guy has lost his mind. I think he knows that we can't afford to lose him right now so he just keeps pushing."

"Don't brush this under the rug. He may be totally harmless but until we figure this out, don't take anything for granted."

"Thanks."

This was not exactly what I wanted to talk about on our first date. I held up a DVD of *The Ugly Truth*. "Have you seen this?"

"No. What's it about?"

"Well, this woman thinks this guy only wants women for their bodies and that he's incapable of a relationship."

"Sounds familiar," London mumbled from behind her glass of iced tea.

I chuckled. "I take offense to that. Just watch."

By the time the couple on the screen were feeling the increase in emotions and were making out in the elevator,

I'd turned London's face to mine and our eyes were locked. Was she feeling this too?

"Talk to me." I traced my thumb along her bottom lip.

"About what?" She tucked her head and kissed my palm. That one gesture set my body on fire.

Sliding my hand around the back of her head, I held her still and brought my mouth to hers, gently coaxing her to open and let me taste her. It was as if I were a kid in high school again, getting his rocks off by making out with a girl on the couch. But kissing London was as intoxicating as Johnnie Walker Blue. Bringing one hand up I inched my fingers down the front of her dress until I felt the taught elastic of her bra. Cupping one breast, I moved the lacy fabric down so that I could feel her in my palm and rub the pad of my thumb over her hardening nipple. I heard the gasp of breath, and it was all the confirmation I needed. I reminded myself to take this slow, but we were adults; second base was taking it slow, right?

Taking my other hand, I slid it under the hem of her dress and moved it up to her back so I could pull her closer to me, moving my fingers up her spine, I felt her stretch like a cat. Any moment I expected her to purr. God, this woman was intoxicating. Moving my hand that was in her bra to the other breast, I repeated my gestures, giving equal attention to this tit. More than anything, I wanted to lower my head and take the firm nipple into my mouth, but that would require breaking our kiss and I didn't know if I possessed the strength to do that.

I hadn't realized how long we'd been kissing until music started playing and the credits from the movie started to roll.

Still, London was the one who pulled away because I couldn't seem to make myself let her go.

"I'd better get going," London said as she glanced at her watch. "It's after ten and sunrise comes all too soon."

I walked her out to her truck, fighting every step of the way not to stop in the middle of the sidewalk and pull her into my arms for another kiss. "I get off at six, want to do something?" I trailed my fingers up and down her back.

"How about you come to my house and hang out with us? That way, it doesn't count as a date."

"I can do that." I pulled her into me when we finally got to the truck and moved my mouth to hers. Wrapping my arms around her, holding her flush against my body. "I'm working the next two days, so let's plan date two for after that, want to say Saturday?" I gave her one more deep kiss then broke our contact so I could open her door for her. She slid in behind the steering wheel and then looked over at me with her lust-filled eyes.

Yeah, not long, London, not long.

I wanted to make up to her for that one night, but once I got her into bed again, I wasn't sure that I'd let her out.

~

THE NEXT DAY, I came up with an idea for date number two, something that would hopefully make London happy and not have her rushing away at ten o'clock.

My plan wasn't something I could pull off by myself, so I enlisted a bit of help.

"Hello?"

"Hi, Paris, this is Braden. I've got a favor to ask."

"Okayyy." She sounded a little apprehensive as she waited for my reply.

"I want to take London out for a picnic Saturday night. I know that she hates being away from the ranch so I figured that we could have a date right there but away from everyone."

"That is so romantic. What were you thinking?"

"A picnic, but I was hoping you would help."

"What do you need?" She sounded far more excited than she had a minute ago, and I grinned.

"Well, I was hoping you would be able to pack the basket for us." Asking her to put together something like that seemed a bit strange, almost as if I should have done it myself so the thought behind the date seemed more authentic, but I didn't have a picnic basket and I didn't have the first clue as to what London would enjoy. Plus, Paris loved cooking.

"We have a big basket I can put together for you. I'll ask Holland to have Mim and Jafar ready, and I'll have the basket set. Do you work that day?"

"No, but I have some errands to do before I head over. I thought that I'd get there around six."

"Leave it to me, she's going to love it. Braden..."

"Yes?"

"Don't hurt her."

"Not planning on it." I disconnected with Paris. I'd told her the truth, hurting London was the last thing in the world that I'd want to do.

I PULLED up to the Kelly Ranch a few minutes after six. I trusted Paris to pack enough food, but I wasn't sure about the other things. So, I'd packed a small blanket, two lanterns, and some bug repellant—this was Florida after all. I had also downloaded some playlists from Spotify. All of that I left in my truck for later.

"Come in, door's open," someone called from inside, but my hand hesitated on the knob. It was just a little weird to be walking in like this. Asher and Marcus didn't bother to knock, but it still felt like intruding.

My only other choice was to stand there like an idiot, so I twisted the knob and entered.

Paris gave me a bright smile as she turned off the stove and then picked up a basket and carried it over to me. Grabbing the basket, I thanked her for organizing everything as well as whatever she'd packed inside. Turning I didn't see Holland to thank her for getting Mim and Jafar saddled and ready as well.

"Will you thank Holland for me? I really appreciate this."

"Of course, now we expect you to keep her out all night."

"I'll try my best. Paris, while we have a second, I wanted to get your take on the whole situation. You seem to be awfully trusting of Ryan."

"Yep, you know why?"

I shook my head.

"Do you know the easiest way to catch a traitor? It is to make them believe that you still trust him."

"What?"

"I don't trust Ryan, but he doesn't know that."

"But your sister—"

"London thinks trust has to be established between employer and workers or it somehow makes us bad bosses. But Ryan was hired by Daddy, so to me, he isn't our employee."

"So, you really think he's doing all of this?"

Paris nodded but didn't answer before she stepped back and smiled at something behind me. I turned, and London took my breath away. She was wearing a pair of dark jeans that graced the curves of her body like they were made for her. Her blonde hair was down again and if it weren't for the fact that she was wearing cowboy boots, I'd think that she was getting ready to model somewhere. The woman was beautiful, and I didn't think she had a clue about her beauty, which made her all the more attractive. She never did any of those hair tosses that so many women did when they were trying to flirt that half the time only sent stray strands floating in your face.

"Good evening." I winked at London, who was smiling, and I knew that I was lost.

"Hey."

"You ready to go?" She stepped forward and reached for me as if she didn't require any coaxing to take my hand in her own.

Leading London outside, I carried the basket, and then grabbed the extra stuff from my truck and took it to the horses where Holland had tied them to the hitching post that was staked along side the house.

"Where are we going? I thought that you were taking me out?"

I ignored London's question. "Do you have an area of the ranch, somewhere that you find peaceful?"

"Yes, I always loved going to that area where my daddy planted tons of palm trees, it reminds me of a little oasis."

"Where I was the other day, where we made the bet?"

"Yeah, that's the one."

We climbed up on the horses and galloped across the open fields. I stayed about a leg behind her just so I could watch the graceful move of her body in the saddle.

Once we were unpacked, I opened the picnic basket and could have kissed Paris for what I found inside. The girl had packed a can of whipped cream and a squeeze bottle of chocolate syrup. I shook my head and laughed since it appeared that she wasn't intending our dessert to just be chocolate chip cookies.

I opened one of the two bottles of wine Paris packed and poured London a glass before pouring one for myself. Turning on some music from my iPhone, we took a seat, and listened.

"Now this is what I call a concert. I'm not sure which is my favorite sound: nature's song of crickets and cicadas or Morgan Evans singing 'I Do.'"

She laughed and tipped her head back, angling herself so that her face shone bright in the setting sun. She looked good, her lips were lightly stained from the wine, and her cheeks still pale pink from the ride over here.

She glanced in my direction and cocked her head at me, sending a strand of hair falling down over her face.

"What?" She smiled.

"Nothing." I shifted a little closer to her. My pulse picked up as I pushed her hair back from where it had fallen, tracing my fingers around the outline of her face. I could feel the chemistry crackling in the air between us, the same as it had been before, but there was something more intense to it.

She let out the softest moan as our mouths met, and I deepened the kiss, pushing my tongue into her mouth and drawing her toward me. It had been almost two months since the night I ran into her at the bar, and I had been dying to feel her next to me again. I pulled her onto my lap, and one of the bottles of wine that her sister had packed for me knocked over as I did so, but it was hard to give a shit when her soft body was pressed against mine.

I fell back against the hard ground, pulling her down on top of me so her hands were on my chest, and her fingers curled around the top of my shirt as we kissed. I was hard, my cock straining against the constraints of my jeans as she moved her hips ever-so-slightly against me. She pushed her fingers through my hair, fisting her hand and tugging slightly, and the pain mellowed to pleasure as she moved her hand over my chest so she could feel my heart thumping through my shirt.

I let my hands stray down her back to her waist. Good god, she felt better than my memory of her. The inward curve of her waist down to her hips, the softness of her skin, the sweet scent of her...it was intoxicating.

I rolled her over, and she giggled and clutched on to my arms as I moved on top of her, sliding my hands up and over her body to push her arms above her head. She wriggled tantalizingly against me as I leaned down to capture her lips before moving over her chin and her neck, letting my teeth play against her throat for a moment.

"Ah..." she groaned, and she arched her back a little to push her hips against mine, her silent permission to continue. I moved back against her, needing to be closer.

My mouth brushed along her collarbone and toward her breasts, and my fingers popped each button on her blouse free.

She wasn't wearing a bra.

Fuck.

I leaned down to take one of her nipples between my lips, teasing it with my tongue, baring my teeth until the bud hardened in my mouth. She clutched my head, holding me in place, as I moved to her other breast, letting my hand come to rest on the softness of her lower belly as I tormented her with my mouth.

The subtle rise and fall of her hips was almost too much. I grazed my fingers over the top of her jeans and looked up to find her eyes, which were darker than they had been moments ago, watching me with an intent I had never seen on her face before. I shifted down the length of her body without dropping her attention and brushed my mouth along the strip of skin just above her pants, and she shuddered with desire.

I undid her jeans and pulled them down her legs, London lifting her hips to make it easy for me. She was wearing a pair of simple black cotton panties underneath, and I brushed my lips against her through them, making sure she could feel me.

The sound she made as I touched her was the hottest thing I'd ever heard, somewhere between a moan and a cry of impatience. I didn't intend to make her wait any longer.

What the lady wants, the lady gets.

I hooked my fingers around the edge and eased them down, and finally I slipped between her thighs, drank in her needy expression one last time, and pressed my mouth against her pussy.

She was already slick with need, my tongue moving easily against her soft flesh. She tasted as good as she smelled, sweet and musky and tempting, and I soon found that I couldn't get enough of her as I sucked softly and tasted every inch of her.

She was writhing beneath me on the cool earth and rocking her hips against my mouth in encouragement, and I pulled her closer. Slipping my hands beneath her ass, I lifted her hips as her hands dove into my hair, almost frantic in her need for me. I was happy to oblige, guiding her close and closer to the edge with my tongue, stroking her clit in long, slow, relentless caresses until she was mindless.

"Oh my god, Braden," she gasped, yanking me away

from her soft flesh and pulling my body on top of hers. "I need you."

My mouth slammed down onto hers in a tangled mess of teeth and tongue and frantic moans as I blindly reached for the basket. Her hands were at my belt, ripping it open and then pulling my button free. By the time she managed to get the zipper down and was nudging my jeans over my hips, I had a condom in my hand and was tearing the package open.

"Hurry," she breathed. "I'm so close..."

"I want to feel you come," I murmured in her ear as I finally...finally slid into her heat.

"Oh my god, you feel so good." She began to rock her hips back against me, and I pushed deep before pulling almost all the way out of her and then thrusting back in. We moved against each other on instinct, as though this was what it had all been building toward all this time. She lifted her head and pressed it against mine, our breath mingling in the air between us, as I moved against her slowly, savoring the feeling of her, of her sweet body beneath mine.

We were lost in our own world of mixed breaths, sweat-soaked skin, and murmured words. I could have spent the rest of my life there, and I would have, had she not tilted her hips, offering me an angle that would let me go deeper.

"Fuck," I groaned against her lips and slowed my pace to long, slow, deep thrusts that had me hanging on close to the edge. I caught her bottom lip between my teeth, and she let out that noise again—the one that sounded more like a growl than anything else, and finally, she came.

She cried out, the sound slicing through the quiet air around us. Her pussy clenched around me, and I was on the verge of joining her, losing myself at any moment.

Yeah...I was never walking away from this shit.

The pleasure coursing through my system as I looked deep into her eyes as she came hard grew and swelled until I couldn't take it any longer and my own pleasure took over.

We both came back down to reality together, and I slowly, reluctantly, slid out of her and disposed of the condom. She was still lying on the ground, staring at the sky with hazy eyes, when I curled up on the blanket next to her.

12

LONDON

There were only a few things in my life that I found addictive. They were—in no particular order—ice cream and horse riding. Braden fucking McManus was just added to that list. He seemed to be the one addiction that I hadn't counted on. Better than having a quart of my favorite ice cream, Ben and Jerry's Chunky Monkey all to myself. And no matter how hard I tried, I was afraid that I wasn't going to get tired of him anytime soon.

"Hey, beautiful, good morning." Braden's deep, smooth voice sent me bolting upright.

"What time is it?" I looked around, trying to get my bearings.

"A little after three."

"Holy shit." We'd been out here for almost nine hours.

"You fell asleep and were sleeping so solid that I hated to wake you."

Shit. My sisters would be up in, like, two hours. I twisted side to side and looked for my shirt, only to find that Braden had slipped it back on me while I slept.

I reached for my boots that were still in a pile at the foot of the blanket, but Braden grabbed them first and handed me one.

"You want to wait for sunrise before we head back?" he asked as he handed me my second boot.

"I wish that I could, but being short-handed I do start my day before sunrise."

"That's okay, I have another date to plan anyway. I want us to go out somewhere." He cupped my face with both hands and brought his mouth down to mine in a kiss that sent shivers to my belly. I knew I needed to hurry; yet, I couldn't seem to get myself to pull away. I wanted to stay right there for a little bit longer but the burden of responsibility was weighing heavily on me.

He pulled back, saying, "I should take you back."

I knew we needed to, but that didn't mean I wanted to. Still, I let him pull me to my feet and helped him collect our stuff.

As we mounted the horses, neither of us seemed to be in a hurry to get back to my place. I was also fairly certain that neither one of us wanted this night to end.

"I CAN'T BELIEVE that you've spent your entire morning here helping me with chores." I leaned back into the crook of Braden's arm as we snuggled on the couch.

"I didn't mind one bit. Kind of liked it, in fact. It was nice seeing what all you do. You three work hard."

"Thanks—"

"I can't believe that asshole!" Holland screeched as she slammed the door shut. She kicked off her cowboy boots and tossed them across the room and then threw her body onto the sofa next to us.

"Care to fill a sister in?" I leaned forward and grabbed the remote to turn off the television.

"Who's an asshole?" Paris stepped into the living room, drying her hands off on a towel.

"Reid Brooks, that's who. He saw me riding Khan, and the asshole starts shouting at me and saying that I need to take better care of my horse, that he looks sick. Then he has the nerve to say that if I can't ride him properly and can't take care of him properly, then I should sell him to someone who can. Are you fucking ready for this? He offered me a price."

I gasped. Holland loved Khan, she loved all the horses and no one took better care of horses than she did.

Before she could answer, the front door opened and Asher walked in. He took one look at all of us standing around and looking pissed and raised one brow as if trying to figure out what the hell was going on. I shook my head.

"You know I find this totally offensive." Holland stomped her foot. "Asshole doesn't think that I know how to treat horses or ride. I should call him and tell him just how wrong he is."

Asher caught my eye, and I mouthed to him, *Reid Brooks*.

"That may not be the best idea. The guy is a jerk, and nothing you say to him will change that."

"You don't trust me to call him and set him straight?" Holland glared at me and I knew that my answer would make this situation either turn catastrophic or start to defuse it.

"Of course I do. I just don't think people like him ever see the reason."

"Him and Ryan deserve each other. Reid is a know-it-all,

and Ryan doesn't trust us to handle our own ranch business. Really? Why do I even stay around? None of y'all needs me." Holland was on a roll.

"Holland, calm down. We need you. The horses need you. And your students need you. You're an awesome equestrian instructor."

"What students?" She threw her hands up into the air. "Neither of my clients showed up today. That's two days in a row without any students, I have no fucking clue what's going on."

"Did you call them?" Braden sat up finally getting invested in our conversation.

"Yes, but I haven't heard back yet." Holland marched to pick up her boots and then headed off to her room.

"Does she always have such problems with your neighbor?"

"Welcome to my life, yes, it is part of an everyday occurrence." I blew my hair out of my face and gave him a tired smile.

"Do you want me to go talk to Reid? Maybe it will help since I'm kind of a neutral party."

"I'm going with you." Holland must have been listening because she came running back down the hall.

"Holland, that defeats the idea of him being a neutral party. Let Braden go alone. You're likely to start a fight with your temper. What you really need to do is call your students and figure out what the hell is going on."

"Fine." She acquiesced but with a ton of reluctance.

I smiled at him. God, it was nice to have him around.

"Promise not to let him get to you?" I asked, already knowing that almost nothing got under Braden's skin, so I didn't need to worry about my uppity neighbor.

"I promise. I'll be back in a bit." He dropped a quick kiss to my lips and then headed out.

When I snapped out of my lusty thoughts about how great his ass looked in jeans, Paris was grinning at me like a fool. "You like him a lot, don't you?"

"I don't know. Maybe if I had a moment to breathe without something happening, I might actually get to analyze my feelings."

"London Kelly, I think that you are blind." Paris whistled as she went back to the work.

I heaved myself up and joined her in the kitchen and grabbed a dishtowel, drying the dishes as she handed them to me. "Yeah, I like him, but he scares me."

"Why in the world does that man scare you? If anything, he should be making you feel secure." Paris continued washing the plates and wasn't paying any attention to me. I was thankful as it gave me time to try and figure out what the hell was going on. But that didn't work out well because the harder I tried to think about it the more my head started pounding, along with my heart. It was like I had just drunk a giant coffee chased by a Monster Energy drink.

"Sure he'd protect me as in not letting anyone or anything harm me physically, but I'm not so sure about emotionally."

"You're worried about your heart?" Paris turned off the faucet and faced me.

"Yeah, I think—" But I didn't get to finish my statement because Braden swung open our front door, and he was followed by one very gorgeous, very pissed off man I had never met before.

Holland came down the hall, and all it took was a single glance at the anger riding her features for me to know exactly who the man was. "You! How dare you bring this...this...asshole into our home." Holland pointed at the man.

"Holland, that's enough." Braden held up both hands. "Why don't you three take a seat? I think you are going to be very interested in what Mr. Brooks has to say."

Paris and I sat without any issue, but Holland looked as if she was trying to decide if throwing something at the man would be a better use of her time. After a second, I grabbed her elbow and tugged her down onto the couch next to me.

To his credit, Reid didn't look all that put out by the scene, and gave each of us a warm smile.

"Hi, I'm sorry that I haven't come over and introduced myself yet, but"—he glanced over at Holland—"someone has done a very thorough job of letting me know that I wasn't invited."

"Humph." Holland crossed her arms and turned her head to look away from him.

"Anyway, Braden told me about what happened to the horses, and I'm sorry. I wish I would have known so I could have helped. My stables aren't full yet and your horses would have been more than welcome to stay there."

"Yeah, for how much?" Holland asked snidely.

"Will you stop acting like some spoiled rotten...I've about had enough from you."

Holland jumped to her feet. "You've had enough from me? You've had enough?"

"Will you let me speak? First, I wouldn't charge anything, which is why I came over. I offered to let your cattle use my property for free as well, all I asked was that you help with the labor since I hadn't hired anyone yet."

"Wait." I stopped Holland before she jumped in. "You offered to let our cattle roam on your land for free? Then where did the eighteen dollars an acre come from?"

"I have no clue, but I never said any such thing. Look, you three have a nice ranch and beautiful stables for Western riding, but that isn't my forte. I'm a breeder and trainer; I deal strictly with thoroughbreds. During the winter months, I house a lot of horses for clients, but during race season, my stables are bare except for my own stock or if I'm training or rehabilitating. I have no problems helping a neighbor out. Despite what some"—he turned his focus on Holland—"think of me, I'm not a bad person. I love animals, and I want to get along with my neighbors."

"I don't get this...why would Ryan lie about this? It doesn't make sense."

"Think about it. Another strain on the checkbook is just another way to hurt the ranch." Braden flexed his fingers and then moved his hands to rest on his hips.

"But we didn't take him up on it, we've just been working around it instead."

"And now other things are happening to ruin the ranch," Braden offered.

"Mr. Brooks—"

"Call me Reid."

"Reid, I'm not trying to start any problems, and you don't have to answer me if you don't want, but did you offer Ryan a job while he was with you?"

"No, ma'am. Poaching other people's employees isn't really something I care to do."

I turned my attention to Holland, and her cheeks were red. Good, maybe she was feeling embarrassed for the way she'd been treating our neighbor.

"I'm getting a drink, anyone want anything? Mr. Brooks?" I fought back my laugh as Holland asked this between gritted teeth. She'd been fine with hating the guy, and she almost looked disappointed that he wasn't the villain she wanted him to be.

Reid, who had been watching her as well, cleared his throat. "I would love to, but I do have to get back. I want you all to know that I meant what I said. You are welcome to use my land, and if you need anything, just holler. I gave my number to your boyfriend here." He nodded to Braden.

I wasn't sure if I liked having Braden referred to as my boyfriend, but I didn't hate it either, so I didn't correct him.

Once Reid left, I knew we had a bigger problem to face —Ryan. He'd lied to us and tried to extort money from us. "Do you think he was planning to take the money and keep it?" I turned to Paris, waiting for her answer.

"I don't know, but I do know that I don't trust him anymore, and I don't want people I don't trust working for us. We should find out if Wally was in on this."

"No. There's no way." I'd never believe that of Wally. He and his wife Ann had been like a second set of parents to us growing up.

"But you said that Wally went with him." Paris was the one being tough, which was a shock since she was the motherly sort.

"Paris, no. We've known Wally our whole lives. He was Dad's best friend."

"Don't care. You need to find out." Paris turned to Braden. "Can you give Ryan one of those no-trespass tickets or whatever?"

He nodded. "Yeah, once London is done, I can issue him a no trespass and enter it into the system just in case he shows back up. You'll need to mail him his final check too."

"That's fine by me."

Holland finally rejoined just as she was hanging up her phone. When she looked toward us, tears were in her eyes.

"That was Ben."

"The fire inspector?" Braden asked.

"Yeah. His daughter missed her riding lesson. Well, he was finally getting back to me, and it seems someone called him and left a message saying that we were suspending lessons indefinitely. He said that he just registered Abbie for another stable and paid the tuition in full, but if anything happens he'll let us know."

"That doesn't make sense, no one called him," I said, completely and utterly confused as to what exactly was going on.

"I know," Holland snapped. "He said it was a man's voice."

"What the fuck?"

"Ryan," Paris chimed in. "What else is that jerk going to try to mess up?"

"Nothing if I can help it." Because the next time I saw Ryan, I was going to have him escorted off the property by Braden. "Holland, call the rest of the parents and check in with them to see if they got the same call. Let them know that it was made in error and lessons haven't been suspended. There is a folder in the top drawer of my desk that has all the students who have inquired about lessons. You can start calling them if there are any openings."

"I'm on it." Holland headed back toward my office.

I bit my bottom lip with a heavy sigh. "This was unbelievable."

Braden pulled out his phone, put it on speaker, and dialed. After a few rings, someone answered.

"This is Ben."

"Hey, it's Braden, I have a strange question for you. By any chance do you still have that voice mail you received from Iron Horse Stables?"

"I think so. If not, it is in my deleted messages and I have thirty days to restore it. Why?"

"Can you do whatever you need to do to retrieve it and then forward it to me? No one from the ranch called you, so we want to add this to the file of weird events that have been occurring."

"You got it. I'm on it now."

Braden and Ben disconnected, and we sat in silence, which was stupid because this could take ten minutes or ten hours.

Thankfully, it took less, because almost as soon as I had the thought, Braden's phone pinged. He hit a few buttons and, once again, put his phone on speaker and set it on the table.

"Hello, Mr. Stinson, I'm calling you from Iron Horse Stables..."

My gut wrenched, and I shoved the edge of my fist into my mouth to hold back any noises.

"I'm sorry to leave this on your voicemail, but we are unable to keep the stables operating at this time. We are hoping that in the near future there will be some changes to the management and that the stables and ranch will return to the smooth operation you once knew. We hope that you are able to find a new training facility for Abbie, and we will notify you if anything changes."

When the message ended, I locked eyes with Braden. He didn't say anything. He didn't have to, there was no tiptoeing around this. We'd all recognized Ryan's voice. We knew that he was the one who left that voicemail.

I jumped and turned at a knock on the front door and then groaned, "What now?"

Braden beat me to the door and opened it to a cocky

looking Ryan facing us. I had to fight back my temper, I wanted to lunge forward and wipe that smirk off his face.

"Afternoon, ladies." Ryan smiled at Braden, probably thinking his comment was a barb.

"Ryan, stay there." I walked to him, refusing to allow him into my home. I felt Braden move to stand at my back. "We spoke with Reid Brooks today, we know about the money and that he wasn't going to charge us to use his fields."

"Bullshit. He said fourteen dollars."

"Interesting, a month ago it was eighteen. Can't you keep your story straight?" I was pissed that he'd tried to take advantage of us after everything my dad had done for him not to mention all the chances we'd given him.

"I don't know, can't remember," Ryan snapped.

"Was that before or after he offered you a job?" I really just wanted to tell him to get the hell off my property, but I knew everyone else needed answers.

"It was before."

"Mmm, crazy thing is that he claims that he *never* offered you a job."

"Obviously, he's lying. He doesn't want you to realize that he tried to steal me away."

"By the way, Ryan, you wouldn't know anything about phone calls being made to Holland's students, would you?" I didn't pay attention to Ryan because I was busy watching Braden.

"Nope, don't know anything about that. What's all this about anyway? You just trying to pin shit on me? Just like a bunch of girls, things start falling apart, and you have to blame someone, that it?"

Braden, to his credit, hadn't decked Ryan yet. No, he was far too smart for that. He just picked his phone up and hit play, smirking as Ryan's voice filled the dead silence swelling around us.

When the message clicked off, I glared at the man my father had trusted for seventeen years.

"Ben sent that a few minutes ago. You know Ben, right? He's the fire inspector who was called out the night the east pasture burned. His daughter was one of Holland's students. Anyway the message was left on his voice mail so he forwarded it to me. Kind of handy since now I can submit it into evidence. Yep, the case just keeps getting stronger. I'll have a voice analyzer on this immediately."

"It isn't against the law to lie." Ryan's smug reply made me want to scratch his eyeballs out.

"No, you're right, but it is against the law to do that stuff over phone lines. You see...that makes it federal jurisdiction. Surprise, you amped up your own charges, and I'll be handing all of this over to State Attorney Conte's office."

"Fuck you." Ryan took a step to leave.

"Stop right there, we aren't done yet. Did you know that trying to get London to pay money that Mr. Brooks didn't ask for is called extortion? That is a felony, and I've added it to the list of things for the state attorney to look into."

I stepped forward, feeling safe with Braden next to me. "Needless to say, you're fired. I'll mail you your final check by certified mail."

"No you won't. I'll come get it." Ryan balled his fists as his face turned a shade of dark red.

Braden stepped around me. "Ryan Cardenas, you are no longer allowed on the Kelly Ranch or Iron Horse Stables. This includes any part of the outlying property, no matter the reason. If anyone should see you here, they've been instructed to call 9-1-1, at which time, you will be arrested for trespassing. Do you understand this?"

Braden waited for Ryan to answer, but my former employee just glared.

"I said, do you understand this? I'm not playing around. This is an official notice and will be entered into the system. Do you understand?"

"Yes."

"Good. Now, you need to leave the property. I'll follow you out." Braden turned to me and whispered, "Stay in here."

13

LONDON

When Braden came back in, he brought Marcus with him, and they looked as if they were so deep in conversation that they wouldn't notice if the world exploded.

"What's going on?" I leaned forward, trying to put my face in front of Braden's to get his attention.

"We're just worried about Ryan coming back and causing more problems. Marcus can be around during the day when I have to work, and Asher in the evenings, but it's during the night I worry about."

"Why don't you stay here?" When he didn't immediately reply, I knew that I'd asked too much. "Well, I'm mean, you are welcome to...any of you are welcome to actually. We have plenty of room."

"That's a good idea, I'll stay." Braden nodded slowly. "I'm not going to leave you three alone,. Between me, Asher, and Marcus one of us will be here for the next few days while the smoke settles around here. I just want to make sure that Ryan gets the hint you three are not to be fucked with."

I looked at my sisters, who both seemed to be in agreement.

"Is that all you two were talking about. You seemed awfully deep in conversation."

"Marcus was telling me about something that happened at the bar. He had an ex employee who had access to his books, and he was wondering how much access Ryan had?"

"None. No one does but me. Not even my sisters, but they know where I keep everything."

"Can we talk in your office?"

"Sure." I felt the unease rising up like acid burning up my throat but I led the way.

"Marcus, you coming?" Braden asked.

"Um, I'm good. I'll let the two of you talk this one out." Marcus gave Braden two thumbs-up.

He followed me back to my office, and I took a seat behind my desk, watching as Braden moved to the safe. He spun the lock a few times, and I heard the telltale sound of the click.

"Hey, wait a minute. How did you know that combination?" I had never opened the safe in front of him, and I knew damn well that I had never told him the combination either.

"London, your safe's combination is the numerical equivalent of your initials—twelve, sixteen, and eight—which isn't very original."

"This is impossible. It could have been anything."

"But it wasn't, which is part of my point." Braden smirked challengingly. "Let's try this." Braden moved the mouse on my computer and then typed something into the password field. I smirked when it told him he'd entered the wrong password. He tried again, and again the little box shook alerting him that he'd entered the wrong passcode.

He tried a third time, and this time, my home screen came up. "Really, London, your passcode is Grimhilde? Wasn't that your first horse?"

"Not everyone knows that." I defended.

"Everyone around here does."

Braden then opened the ranch files that held the payroll and profit and loss records. I smiled because I didn't think he knew my email address, and he'd have to enter it as a login and a password.

Braden moved the mouse to the bottom toolbar and clicked on the mail icon, opened it, and then clicked on the first email that popped up. He copied the email address that it was addressed to, which was mine—damn it all to hell—and then pasted that into our bookkeeping program.

"London, never use your regular email address for any logins. Whether it be this program, your bank, or Facebook. Hackers have to figure out both of these and your email is the ranch's email address, it's way too easy and you made their job even easier."

Then just as methodically as he did with the code to the computer, he began trying combination after combination until he was granted access.

"What's your point to all of this?" I was still dazed by the fact that he had opened the locks and gained access as easy as one, two, three, and my life...our livelihood was ripe for his picking. This was just one more thing to add to the list to prove that I couldn't do what my dad had done, I wasn't fit to run the ranch.

"I'm just doing my job."

I snorted. "I don't think that a deputy's job requires cracking codes or invading privacy."

"No, you're right. I'm talking about my job as your boyfriend and someone who cares. If I can help, I will. I just wanted to show you that, just like Marcus's ex-employee, Ryan could have gotten your information. You sent him home for his attitude and you moved Wally into a lead position, so he had to suspect something was coming, and as such he may have been gathering information just in case you finally did fire him. Please let me help. What I'm doing will help you. It will show you where you need to tighten your security."

"No it isn't. It's showing me that I'm incompetent. That I've opened myself up to being robbed blind or whatever." I hit the tape dispenser when I swung my hand out to emphasize my point, and it crashed to the floor. I left the damn thing there. "So when Marcus brought this up, you knew immediately that you better check mine huh? Odds were a stupid female like me wouldn't know how to keep her shit safe, is that what you're saying?"

"No, nothing like that. I'm not sure why Marcus is here but he pulled up as I was escorting Ryan out. One thing led to another, and we got to talking about making sure the three of you were safe."

"So you discussed my safe and computer password?"

"No, nothing like that. Will you stop jumping to conclusions? I was getting Marcus up to speed about the phone calls to the students. He asked me if I was sure that was all he'd found access to, your student records. His former employee got access to all of his—"

"Yeah, I know what she did, Marcus and I are friends, remember?" I was getting pissed because he was treating me like a child. "She logged into his business accounts from her home and was changing his alcohol orders. It took several weeks to figure it out, but by that point, the bar was hurting because each week their deliveries were off, and Marcus was pissing off customers because the trucks wouldn't have the right stuff."

"Exactly. Nothing like being a bar that runs out of beer. Marcus mentioned your safe and that you did all of your business online as well. He brought it up so that you didn't upset Holland's clients."

"Too late for that."

"But more than that, once he mentioned it I wanted to make sure that you didn't have everything you have worked so hard for stolen."

I swore under my breath. "Who do you think you are? This is not your problem. You're a sheriff, you investigate then you go home, the rest of it is my and my sisters' job. Not yours. Your last name isn't Kelly. Contrary to whatever you think about Ryan and his highhanded ways, you're acting just as bad." I was fuming. There was no way that I'd let him make me feel so...so...inadequate—even if he was freaking right. I didn't need saving, I could save myself, I'd been doing it for the last thirty years without him, and I'd keep doing it without him. "What makes you think that I want you interfering in my business or that I need you meddling? Whatever gave you that hint? Nothing did, you're just assuming that I can't do it."

"Clearly, that isn't the case if I can walk into this office and get access to all of your information, London. You're pissed because I pointed out a weakness in your system that you didn't see. There isn't anything wrong with that, and I would do it again if it meant keeping your business safe from assholes like Ryan. Who, by the way, I am nothing like and you know it." .

"Oh, really? From what I can tell you're a chauvinistic, man whore who thinks woman are incompetent playthings. You and Ryan have a lot in common. Guess what, asshole, the game's over. You might be a player, but you just met the umpire and I'm calling strike." I cursed at the tears that were building up in my eyes.

"If you truly feel that way about me after everything, then I guess there's no need for me to hang around." Braden looked baffled and shocked before he turned on his heel and strode from the room. A minute later, the sound of the front door opening and shutting echoed through the house. I wiped the traitorous tear that streamed down my cheek. I wasn't upset that he left. I was livid that he would act this way. My blood was boiling. How dare he try to invade my life like he had the right to.

Burying my face in my hands, the smell of vanilla filled the air and without looking up I knew it was Paris. She never wore perfume, and there was no need since no matter how much she wore, she'd always smell like fresh baked cookies. Paris entered my office and then moved to stand next to me, her soft hand gently rubbing my back. The hum of the ceiling fan as it circled was the only sound that flooded the otherwise silent room.

When I finally raised my head, Paris was staring at me with sympathetic eyes. "He left, he couldn't get out of here fast enough. As soon as he realized that I was pissed which meant he just blew his chance of getting into my pants for the night he was out of here. He's probably flipping through his black book of skank whores right now, trying to figure out who he can get to replace me."

"Well, then good riddance." Paris wiped her hands like she was sweeping off the dirt. "If he can replace you so fast then we want him gone. How dare he do that to you? I'm going to call him right now and tell him just what I think of him. How dare he leave here and immediately call another woman. Fuck him. You don't need him. What's his number?"

Paris reached for my phone and pulled it to her but I heard the crack in her voice as she fought back her laugh.

"Don't do that."

"But you think it is. And if you think he's that kind of man then you shouldn't waste another second on him. That means he was only after one thing and I had him pegged all wrong. Just you wait until I tell Asher and Marcus."

"I didn't mean don't call him, I meant don't keep acting like an idiot, I get your point. You're making fun of me."

Paris threw her hands against her chest and let out a mock gasp. "Who me? Never."

"Yeah, whatever. You've made your point."

"Which point would that be, the one that made you listen to how crazy you were sounding or the one that made you realize that Braden is not that kind of man? But I love you no matter what, even when you act a little psycho."

Damn Braden. Damn that Braden fucking McManus. Damn him for making me so mad. Damn him for making me lose my temper. Damn him for making me want him and then acting so heavy handed.

"Why did I say all those things to him? I hadn't meant to hurt him, but he made me feel useless, and I just lost it. Why in the world can't I control my temper around him?"

"We're always harder on those we love the most," Paris said softly.

Love. Love Braden? Did I love Braden? Holy shit, I did. Crap, I was in love. I loved him, and I had just run him off.

"Oh my god, what am I going to do?" I tucked my head into my hands and grabbed hold of my hair, ready to yank it out. "He's never going to talk to me again. He was so pissed when he left. I said horrible things."

"Give him some time, let him cool down and then call him."

I wasn't sure that he'd forgive me—hell, I wasn't sure that I'd forgive me. I regretted everything that had transpired earlier but right now I think I was just too tired to handle all of it. I was emotionally drained. In the span of a day, I discovered that Ryan had been trying to extort money from us as well as ruin us by calling the students. Not to mention Braden believed that Ryan was the one who started the fire and poisoned the horses.

I also needed to figure out how to protect my family from being hacked or robbed—good god, I was failing, and Dad had only been gone a few months. To top it all off, I was in love. Worse yet, I had just chased that love away. Please tell me that this was the bottom of the barrel because I wasn't sure that I could handle any more.

"Thanks, Paris. I'll give him a call in the morning and apologize. Right now, all I want to do is go to bed and forget today ever happened."

"You and me both, you and me both."

When I stood, she gave me the type of hug only a sister could give, and waited around until I'd locked the office before heading to the kitchen as I headed toward my room.

All the while, I thought about how I'd been the biggest kind of fool.

14

LONDON

Leaning on the split rail of the fence that lined the cattle pasture, I replayed the past few months of my life and how everything had gone pear shaped. I needed to talk to Braden and apologize, but the truth was that I was too chicken to pick up the phone when he had called last night.

Maybe, I was just too scared to find out that he wouldn't forgive me for what I'd said. Telling myself that Braden was on shift and there was no use calling him tonight anyway, I made a promise to myself that I'd call him tomorrow. Yeah, that was what I'd do. He wouldn't have time to speak to me anyway. I'd call him first thing tomorrow and apologize.

Heat lightning flashed across the horizon, and I loosed a deep, cleansing breath. I loved this time a day when night was just starting to fall. I knew that it was nothing more than regular old lightning far off in the distance, but I always associated it with the evening time since that was when it was easiest to see.

Taking a deep breath, I inhaled saltiness and knew that the storm was headed our way. Needing to get a few things done before calling it a night, I walked back to the barn and stopped to see Mim. Grabbing a few apples, I remembered what Holland had said about the horses knowing I played favorites, so I put the apples back into the bag and picked up the whole thing instead. As I walked down the row, I handed each one a tart treat. "Here you go, Ursula, Shere Khan, Tremaine, and Gaston." One after one they poked their heads out of their stalls to be greeted and give a neigh at getting a snack.

Finally reaching the end, I pulled out the last two apples and gave one to Balthazar and then turned and gave the last one to Mim. "Hi, beautiful girl, how you doing? Are you ready to get brushed?" She stuck her head out and I gave her the apple, trailing my fingers lightly down her muzzle while she ate, before heading into the tack room to grab her brush. Heading out of the main part of the stables to the back, I was stopped by two strong arms. They grabbed me—one clasped over my mouth and the other wrapped around my waist—and then I was yanked against a hard chest. In a fight or flight reaction, I jerked to pull away as the fear flooded my bloodstream.

"Don't make a fucking sound. I'm tired of your bullshit. It is time that I show you exactly what women are supposed to do, and that is service men."

Ryan pulled his hand away from my mouth and slid it to his pocket. "How dare you—"

"Uh-uh, I told you to shut up, but you didn't listen did you?" He pushed me to the ground, and I swung my arms out, reaching for him. "You make this so much more fun." He pulled out a bandana from his front pocket and tried to shove it into my mouth, but I held my lips firmly closed. His heavy body straddled mine, his weight pressing down on my chest as he leaned forward to restrain my arms and pin them down with his knees. When he squeezed my nostrils shut, I bucked, trying to get him off me, but he won and it was either open my mouth to breathe or pass out.

Being unconscious was the last thing I wanted. He shoved it in. I tried to spit the disgusting cloth out, but it was no use, he wrapped another one around my head and tied that one at the back of my skull.

Grabbing both wrists, he tied them together with a lead rope that we used for the horses and then dragged me back to Holland's office. Wrapping the rope around the legs of Holland's heavy desk, it kept me low to the ground. I kicked and twisted my body as he grabbed my left ankle and wrapped a lead around it and pulled it tight. He did the same to my right ankle before he stretched me out, tying one leg to a beam and the other to a hook on the wall to my left.

Think, London, think.

Hands, hands, my hands were my best bet to get free. If I could pull the desk and maybe slide the rope under the leg, I would be free. Was there an uneven paver, anything? Fuck, Holland and Paris were asleep, but I hoped they would wake up to come check on me.

I whimpered and shuddered as Ryan trailed his fingers over me, his hands were cold and the grin on his face dissolved all the strength I had as tears began rolling down my cheeks.

"You really like pissing me off, don't you?" I shuddered as Ryan trailed a knife along my body. "Oh, don't be scared, I'd never hurt you. I don't want to scar your perfect body. After all, I need to look at you when I fuck you for the next fifty years. I'm just going to remove this stupid shirt. You won't need it anymore. I like my women naked when I fuck them," he whispered into my ear then licked the skin down to my neck.

I felt the tug on the material as he lifted it away from my skin and began sawing back and forth with the knife. His hands were cold, and his grin was mocking.

Tears slid from the corners of my eyes and went down my cheeks as his mouth closed around my nipple. I had never imagined being touched by a twisted guy like him and I wished I could crawl out of my damn skin. I didn't want it anymore.

I told myself over and over that this was not happening.

"Plzzz." I didn't even recognize the word escaping my mouth, I knew that there was no way he could understand me with this bandana shoved in my mouth, but I had to plead anyway. "Please don't do this."

He then turned his attention to my jeans, the denim proving more difficult than the thin cotton of my T-shirt. He hacked them to shreds until he could lift them away from me, leaving me in only my panties. The small speck of hope I had that he would leave them on was snuffed out when the edge of the knife sliced through first the left side and then the right before he pulled them away.

I was lying bare for him to take his fill. I continued pleading but quickly realized that my pleading was turning him on. More than once, I had to choke back the vomit that threatened to come up.

He trailed his tongue down my neck, and it sent a shiver of revulsion down my spine.

I whimpered and tried to kick, but I couldn't move more than an inch.

"There's no point in trying to move, darling. All you'll do is hurt yourself." He trailed one finger down my bare chest.

Ryan's mouth continued its journey down my throat.

Yanking on my hands, I endured the pain from the leads rubbing, cutting, burning into my skin, hoping that my forceful movements would break the ropes bound around me. I wouldn't let him do this, not ever.

It was weird what went through your mind at a time like this. He was towering over me, and I held my eyes shut because I didn't want him to see the fear in them. But in my mind, I had an entire motivation convention going on.

No matter what happens, I will get through this. I will not let this change me. I am not defined by what he does to me.

Over and over I repeated the inspirational, psychological, mumbo jumbo.

15

BRADEN

I sat on the side of State Road 46 and clocked cars, trying to catch speeders. Well, pretending to try to catch people speeding. My mind was out of it and this was pretty much as brainless a job as I could do. Hold, aim, clock. I missed being able to stop by the ranch and see London and eat Paris's cooking. I had figured she needed some time to calm down and then she would realize that I had only been trying to help, but it had been two days and she hadn't called. She also hadn't returned my calls.

All because I wanted to show her that she needed to tighten her security.

Holy fuck, what was wrong with women? They had so much damn pride even when I wasn't challenging it.

My phone rang, and I traded the radar gun for my cell and accepted the call.

"Hello?"

"Howdy, matey?"

"David, you need to lay off the *Pirates of the Caribbean*, it's getting out of hand. What's up?"

"Just checking in on you. Where you at?"

"Running radar on 46, then going to check on the ranch."

"Is she talking to you yet?"

"Not yet." I gritted my teeth as my grip on the phone tightened.

"Any clues at all? Have Marcus or Asher seen anything?"

"No, and that's what is driving me crazy. I know that it's only been two days, but Ryan doesn't seem like a plotter. He's a hot head, which means that it won't be long before we know his next move."

"Okay, well, if you hear anything, will you let me know?"

"Will do." I disconnected and then put my phone into the cup holder, started my engine, and headed to London's house.

When I pulled into her driveway, I cut my lights and rolled to a stop on the side of the long drive just before the curve that faced their house. Sliding my phone onto my tool belt, I locked up my truck and started walking.

The house was dark, but that wasn't surprising since it was so late, but as I headed around the house, I noticed a light on in the stables, which they never left on since Horse's eyes were so sensitive. Watching my step, I stayed close to the brush, and without taking my eyes off the stables ahead, I moved closer only glancing down occasionally to make sure that I wasn't going to trip on a branch or step into a hole.

I heard a noise, like the sound of something falling. Pulling my Glock from my holster, I pressed the button on my radio to call into dispatch. I couldn't explain it but something wasn't right. Trusting my instincts had saved my life more than once in this line of work, so I wasn't about do something different now. "This is Eleven-Eighteen, give me a ten-thirty-eight, ten-forty-six at Kelly Ranch. Have them fifty-six me at the stables."

Turning my volume down so that it was near a whisper, I waited for dispatch to reply. "Seminole County Copies, 11:23 hours, copy."

I released the button.

Taking in the scene in front of me, I tried to go through what I knew of the building in my head. Large main stable, twelve individual stalls, back area with open tack room, and one office that has its own side entry door.

A few deep breaths, I hurried my pace, trying to stay out of the ray of the moonlight and stick close to the building's shadow as I edged around the corner. I was trained to react under pressure, but when it was the person you loved who was possibly at risk, sometimes all training seemed to fly out the window. I got closer, and it was as though an icy hand reached up and grabbed me, I was frozen when a large figure moved in front of a side window. Recognizing that area as Holland's office, all signs were whipping a fucking red flag right in my face. This was bad news since whoever was moving around inside had intentionally not turned the lights on in the office and if someone was in the main part of the stables the two were about to run into each other.

I slowed my breathing as I pressed closer to the window and listened. My chest pounded from anxiety.

I heard a whimper of someone in pain. Then the weight of what felt like fifty bricks landed in my stomach when it hit home that it wasn't just someone, that was London who had whimpered. I had no clue how truly strong I was until that moment when being strong for her was my only choice. It was funny, once you figure out who you want to spend the rest of your life with, you want the rest of your life to start that very moment.

Hearing her whimpers, but not being able to see her or go inside until backup arrived was a whole new kind of torture, one that I'd never experienced before. I probably only stood there one or two minutes, but it felt like one or two hours as I listened to my heart beat and sweat trickle down my face as I tried to make a plan. Deciding that I couldn't wait any longer because London needed me, I made my way around to the giant front doors of the stables.

Bringing my pistol close, I held it at the low ready and then stepped into the well lit main area. The first thing I did was cut the lights. Once the stable was shrouded in darkness, I stepped back outside to safety and to give my eyes time to acclimate and to see if anyone noticed the change.

Once I felt it was safe and I didn't hear anything, I waited about another thirty seconds, then headed back in, this time closing the barn doors behind me. Just in case whoever was back there with London wasn't working alone, the last thing I needed was their partner in crime to sneak up on me. Likewise, I didn't want Paris or Holland realizing that London was missing and then come traipsing into the stables without my knowing.

With my back pressed against the wall, I squatted as I quickly moved under each half door of the stalls and looked around corners to see if anyone else was hiding in here as I tried to secure the front part of the stables where the horses were housed and deem it empty.

Once I was confident that it was just me in here, I stood, and made my way carefully toward that back office, stopping just outside the doorway. There was another muffled cry and then heavy footfalls. Footfalls that were far too loud to belong to London.

All the possible scenarios crashed through me, making

my head swim as each one ended worse than the one before it. I battled through them, knowing that there could be a chance I was over reacting.

Still, I raised my hand and knocked on the closed office door hollering, "London, you in there? I'd like to talk." Before I moved to try the handle, which was locked as I had suspected.

The sounds from the other side of the door ceased, and the silence in the room was the scariest sound of all.

16

LONDON

B raden, please...please.

I sent silent prayer after silent prayer that he'd be able to figure out what was going on.

I tried to yell, but my words were muffled by the bandana and then were totally cut off when Ryan pressed his hand over my mouth. By the time he lifted it there were no more sounds of tapping and no more shouts outside the door. Please, Braden, I began my ritual of silent prayers all over again.

When Ryan's hands rubbed over my belly, he seemed transfixed, almost lost. Then I heard what had caught Ryan's attention. He hadn't been transfixed; he had been concentrating on the sound.

"London? Are you okay?" Braden said before he knocked on the office door.

Ryan froze, and for once, I saw an ounce of fear in him, a sign of desperation, and it scared me just as much as his demented mind. He crooked one finger and placed it under my chin and locked his eyes on mine. When he looked at me, the fear had been replaced with resolve and a smirk.

I let my eyes follow his movements as he trailed a hand to the back of his jeans and pulled out a revolver.

Oh, god.

I shuddered when he leaned closer once more, one hand resting on the desk the other next to my head. "If you make a sound, I'll kill him and then I'll go inside and kill Paris and Holland."

"London, open up. I'm not leaving until we talk." Braden's voice was full of determination.

Ryan moved toward the door as he unbuttoned his shirt then ran his fingers through his hair a few times so that it was disheveled. With one hand, he unsnapped his jeans and then lowered the zipper. He didn't so much as glance back in my direction before he unlocked the door and stepped outside, shutting the door behind him.

When the door shut, I wiggled, using the smooth surface of the pavers to help slide my weight around since my constraints were so tight. Something loosened, I wasn't sure what, but I could move a little more. A warm trickle of blood slid down my wrist, but it was a small price to pay for what I'd gained. I yanked harder, trying to wiggle free, and lifted until I felt the rope catch underneath the leg of the desk. Then I lifted against and again and again until my muscles burned from the effort and the rope holding my wrists loosened.

I could bring my arms to me.

Quickly, I worked on the knots as I listened to the lies Ryan was spilling.

"Deputy McManus, do you know what time it is?"

Braden wasn't stupid. He'd be able to tell that Ryan was obviously trying to hide something.

"I'm here to check on London. I know she's in there."

"Yes, but she can't come out, umm, we're a little busy, if you know what I mean."

"But you were issued a no trespass."

"That is no longer valid since London invited me here."

A lie Braden would see right through. No one claimed Ryan was very smart.

While the two carried on, I continued working on trying to free myself.

Really, Ryan? Slip knots? What, were you expecting a quick getaway?

I snorted but pinched my lips closed as I freed my hands and then started working to free my ankles, which was difficult with my legs spread apart. Pressing my hand to the ground, I pushed myself up and used my other hand to quickly unfasten the ties and still listen to what was going on outside.

His half-baked plan was failing fast, and the only thing he accomplished was pissing me off and adding assault to his ever-growing list of charges.

He would end up in jail for a very, very long time...well, that was if I didn't kill him myself first.

The last knot on my ankle unraveled, and I scrambled to pull a saddle blanket off a shelf and wrapped it around me.

"Ryan, I'm not leaving until I hear from London. You are trespassing, and unless she comes to the door and tells me she invited you onto the property, I have no option but to put you under arrest. So I suggest you get her right now."

He didn't believe Ryan's act to try to make him jealous. God, I didn't deserve this man. He believed in me.

"Actually, she can't come and see you, she hasn't gotten dressed yet, she's still basking." Ryan let out a whistle that made me curse.

"London! Are you inside? Answer me and tell me you're

fine. Ryan, you'll need to step away from the building. You need to come out here with me until I establish you have a right to be here."

Braden's voice was loud enough to echo across the entire ranch. His tone was firm, totally unwavering. I was tempted to open my mouth, but Braden had no idea that Ryan was armed and I had no idea if Braden had his weapon on him.

"Ryan, I'm not going to ask you again, step away from the door and put your hands where I can see them."

I froze as Ryan rushed back inside and tried to slam the door at the same time Braden shoved his body against it. Everything seemed to happen in lightening speed. I filled my lungs with air as Ryan reached for me with one hand.

"You fuckin' bitch!" Ryan yelled. "If you had only agreed to date me, I wouldn't have had to resort to this. We could have been happy. You wouldn't have had to worry about the ranch." Ryan pulled out the revolver from behind him.

He didn't even get it pointed before Braden shot, Ryan crumpled to the ground, and a barrage of officers swarmed in. Shouts echoed from outside, I thought they were my sisters', but the sound of the gun was still echoing in my ears, and I couldn't tell.

"You should have said yes, London. Your dad wanted me to run the ranch, not you, not some stupid girl."

Braden stepped forward and kicked the gun out of Ryan's reach.

I turned to Braden, who had left Ryan to the supervision of the other deputies and pulled me into the safety of his arms. "Sweetheart, look at me." Braden cupped both sides of my face and tried to pull me out of the small stable office. He pressed small rapid kisses on the top of my head as he hugged me in tighter against him. "Are you hurt any where? Paramedics are on their way, we'll have them look at you."

"No, I'm fine." I looked over Braden's shoulder to where Ryan lay. One of the deputies had tied his ankles and blood was flowing from his right arm and dripping onto the stone pavers. With quivering hands, I grasped hold of Braden's shirt, trying to find something to say. "Paris and Holland, are they safe?"

"Yes, they're safe."

"Is he going to die?" I stole another glance back at Ryan, who looked like he'd passed out.

"He'll be fine. I only shot him in the arm and the paramedics are almost here." Braden assured me. "Please, come with me, let's get out of the way."

Braden held on to the blanket, ensuring that I didn't accidentally let go of it, which was smart since I had nothing on underneath, and tugged me outside and over to where my sisters stood.

"I need clothes," I said between chattering teeth. I had no clue why I was shivering, but I was. I wasn't even cold.

Braden pressed a button on his radio and spoke, "I'm taking London Kelly up to her house so that she can gather some clothes. I'll have paramedics examine her there."

With his arm around me, I took one tentative step, feeling the sharp edges of the gravel press into my bare feet. I didn't even really have time to flinch before Braden was scooping me into his arms and carrying me up the long drive. There was no way he was going to carry me, not all the way up to the house. It was a good distance and hilly. But he did, only wobbling every once in a while when his boot landed on a large rock.

I sat in the waiting room.

I hated being here, especially since he tried to rape her.

I met David's eyes as he stood at the opposite end, waiting for word from the doctor. I wasn't in any big hurry since I knew that I was going to be put on a leave of absence, it was standard protocol when you were forced to shoot someone. The investigation would come back in my favor, but I wasn't looking forward to the counseling I would have to sit through. I didn't feel an ounce of guilt for taking that shot.

David leaned forward and pointed to the older woman in a white coat walking toward us and I stood straighter as she stopped in front of me.

"It is my understanding that Mr. Cardenas will be under watch and as soon as he is well, he will be transported to Seminole County jail, is this correct?"

"It is. Do we have an update?"

"Ryan Cardenas is in surgery. Due to his blood type, there are several precautions we need to take."

I nodded, not really caring about whatever complication they were facing.

"Blood type? What sort of precautions?"

"Mr. Cardenas has B negative blood, it is one of the rarest type of bloods, but more than that, those with B negative tend to be more susceptible to autoimmune problems, so we just want to take precaution that he doesn't leave here, only to get an infection somewhere else."

"Well, the physician at the jail will be in touch with you, I'm sure he knows how to get in touch with the hospital and get all of the information but I'll relay everything just to be positive," I assured the doctor.

"Has anyone gotten ahold of Mary Cardenas? She's listed as his emergency contact in our records."

"That was his mother. I believe that she passed away about fifteen years ago."

"How about his father? I'd like to find him, maybe he'd be willing to come in and donate some blood to help restock our B negative storage."

"I'm sorry, but I don't have a clue who that is, I'll ask around and see if anyone knows anything."

"Please let me know if you do."

I reached out one hand to thank the doctor but was stopped in the process by Wally's heavy breathing as he rush toward me and interrupted my saying goodbye to the doctor. Beads of sweat trickled down his face that was etched with concern.

"How's Ryan?" Wally's voice quivered as his eyes glistened with tears.

"This is the doctor." I swung one arm so Wally could meet her.

"I'm sorry, sir, but I can only speak to family or, in this case, the law enforcement."

"I'm his father."

I stepped back, mouth agape.

"Well, then, as you know, there are precautions we take when someone has B negative blood."

Wally shook his head. "No, I don't know about anything about blood, what kind of precautions?"

The doctor pulled the chart away from her chest, flipped it open, and read for a moment as a line of concentration formed on her brow.

"Sir, do you know your blood type?"

"I'm O positive, I think that it's pretty common."

Again, she turned to the file, flipping back and forth through the pages before she slowly closed it and offered him an apologetic look. "Sir, I'm sorry. I can't discuss this with you. I can only discuss Mr. Cardenas's health situation with—"

"I know, you told me. I'm his father. As much as I hate to admit it, he is my son."

"Sir, he can't be your son, not if you are positive that your blood type is O positive. His mother Mary Cardenas also had O positive, so Ryan's father had to have B blood type. I'm sorry." The doctor turned and faced me, but my head was still reeling. "If you'll excuse me, gentleman."

It was all she said before she marched back through the swinging double doors.

I looked at the older man. "Wally, I'm not sure what's going on but I think that you have some explaining to do."

"This is going to sound pathetic, but I had an affair with Ryan's mother. Then, when Ryan was seventeen, his mother died and he contacted me, claiming I was his father. At first, I didn't believe him, but he threatened to go to my wife and daughters. My daughters may be grown and married, but it would devastate them to learn that their dad had cheated on their mom. Not to mention what it would do to Ann. I don't know if any of them would forgive me. So I agreed to meet with him, and well...he made me believe him. I truly thought that I was his father. That was why Sam gave him a job at the ranch. He decided that it would be best to keep Ryan close so we could keep an eye on him. In all these years, I'd never seen this cruel side to him. Sure, I'd seen him get jealous but never cruel."

I nodded, trying to process the bomb he just dropped.

"He may not be my son, but I don't want him to die."

"Don't worry, Wally. He isn't going to die. You can sort things out with him later, after he's been booked and processed."

Wally raised his head and nodded his understanding. "I feel really bad for betraying the girls. I don't know how I'll ever face them. I thought I was his father. He's been blackmailing me, told me I had to help him. I hurt the girls because I was too damn scared to own up to something I did years ago. Their dad was my best friend, and he trusted me to watch over them."

"Wally, I'm not going to lie to you, I have no clue what they'll say but neither do you until you tell them the truth. It's better to do it sooner rather than later."

David, who had been holding his silent post against the wall, agreed to stay to and monitor Ryan's condition while I followed Wally to the ranch.

LONDON, her sisters, and Asher were waiting for us as we pulled up.

"Is everything okay? Wally, are you all right?" London asked, concern filling her eyes.

He wrapped her in a giant hug, tears streaming down the old man's face. "There's something I need to tell all of you, and you might not look at me the same when I'm done—"

"Let's all go inside." I placed a hand on Wally's shoulder and guided him inside.

Once everyone was seated, Wally clasped his hands on his lap and repeated everything he had told me in the hospital. As he did, I kept a close eye on London, my strong, beautiful girl. I knew her heart was breaking, but she sat and listened.

"Fifteen years ago, Ryan came to me with what I considered proof that I was his father." Paris and Holland didn't say anything, but the look on London's face looked as if someone had just told her dog died. "When your father died, something in Ryan changed, he became resentful of people who had parents that left them things. He and his mother lived paycheck to paycheck, barely making ends meet so she had nothing to leave him. And well, Ann and I had the girls, it isn't exactly like I was stepping up to claim him. Anyway, one day Ryan came to me and said that he was in love with you. Truth be told, I didn't think much of it. I told him to ask you out and see what you said."

Wally looked pleadingly to London, clearly hoping she would understand, but she wouldn't meet his eyes, and a part of me felt sorry for the old man.

"I think Ryan got desperate." Wally continued. "Not too long ago, Ann visited here, and Ryan approached her for the first time and asked her if she ever wished she'd had a son. Then he started calling my house, stopping by my house, he had me on pins and needles and I saw my world crashing around me. I couldn't lose Ann or our girls. We have the grand-babies, my daughters would take their mother's side, and I'd never see any of them again." Wally pulled on the front of his shirt as if trying to get some air.

"I don't get it, Wally, what is it you are apologizing to us for? Sounds to me like you should be apologizing to Ann and your daughters." London picked up her mug of coffee and stood, ready to walk off.

"I allowed him to blackmail me. Every time you threatened to fire him or the time you sent him home, he'd dangle his damn birth certificate over my head until I agreed to intervene on his behalf. Then when we went to meet with Mr. Brooks, he asked to speak to Mr. Brooks privately. At first I was against it, but I allowed him to manipulate me and convinced myself that it was okay. I mean, what did it matter? They were only talking about land."

I looked at Holland, who looked angry, and Paris, who looked sad.

But London, she still appeared devastated. Trust meant everything to her, and he'd broken it. She still loved him, which was probably why she had fallen silent. She knew as well as I did that if she said something, she may regret it tomorrow.

"Wally," I said, trying to sound as understanding and non-judgmental as I could, "why don't you head home for a bit. I'll call and let you know about Ryan once we hear something. Give London and her sisters a few days, okay?"

"Yeah, okay." He dropped his shoulders, cast one last look to each of the girls, and then walked out.

LONDON

Braden and I sat in the middle of my bed. I stared at him and realized that he was my home. This man, who I'd thought was just out to use women, had become my safe place, my protector.

"Are you okay?" He leaned forward and tucked that damn lock of hair that always seemed to be falling in my face behind my ear.

"Yeah, just a lot to take in all in one day. I truly never thought that Ryan could be capable of this kind of stuff." Knowing that Ryan was safely behind bars was comforting but also knowing that he'd been the one to cause all the catastrophes was heartbreaking.

"Well when the investigators got to his house and found trace elements of oleander and the university lab confirmed that was what was used on the horses, he confessed to everything. I think that he was hoping for a lighter sentence but the truth was, the guy's house looked like he hadn't done laundry in a year. Forensics scanned enough pieces to find all the evidence they needed to for a slamdunk case. Not to mention the shirt that had holes in it from having lighter fluid spilled on it and then not washed especially since it was finally ruled as the accelerant that started your pasture fire."

"Am I a terribly bad person if I don't want to talk about this anymore?"

"No, I wouldn't blame you one bit. You've been through enough. So what would you like to talk about instead?" Braden bounced on the bed and wiggled his eyebrows.

I stood and moved away from him. "Will you stay the night?" My words were softer than normal, but truthfully, I didn't want him to say no.

"There's no place I'd rather be."

Turning the lock on my bedroom door before returning to where Braden still sat. I took several slow deep breaths as I neared him, he stood, forcing me to stretch up onto my tippy toes. Wrapping one hand into the folds of his shirt, I pulled him close to me. "Kiss me."

"London, you should rest. Today has been exhausting, you've spent hours at the sheriff's station going over all the reports."

"I don't want to rest."

He drew in a deep breath and moaned, "Will you respect me in the morning?" He laughed.

"Hell yes, I will!"

The cool wood against my back was strangely soothing. Maybe it was because I was burning up for this man. He had me all kinds of hot and bothered. With one of his strong hands on my chest, he held me firmly in place. Slipping my arms around his neck, I gently dragged my nails over the nape of his neck. He closed his eyes and let out a small groan of pleasure, as though this was all he'd ever wanted. "Let me see what I can do to make you groan even louder." Planting slow kisses on his lips, I worked my way down his body before falling to my knees in front of him. Parting my lips and shooting a look up at him, I fumbled with the buckle of his pants before pulling them down his legs. I ran my hands over the bulge in his underwear, tracing my nails over his swiftly growing erection. He reached down to push my hair back from my face so he could look me in the eyes. Licking my lips playfully, I exaggerated each motion as I trailed the tip of my tongue over my bottom lip. Slipping my fingers under the waistband of his boxers, I let them fall to the ground, freeing his impressive length, and then immediately wrapping my hands around him and stroking him a few times.

"Fuck, London," he groaned, and I loved the way my name sounded coming out of his mouth. I wanted him as badly as I did that first time we'd been together. I closed my eyes, parted my lips, and leaned forward, flicking my tongue over his tip before I moved to take as much of him into my mouth as I could. He tasted salty as I coaxed him deep into me and ran my tongue over the underside of his cock. When I began to work up and down, enveloping him in the warmth of my mouth, he started to move with my motions. I had no intention of making him finish—no, I was going to get mine too—but I loved how powerful I felt, pleasuring him like this and having him completely at my mercy.

His hands cupped the back of my head, and he began to thrust in slow, shallow movements, and still letting me set the pace. His body tensed with desire as I went down on him. Before I knew it, I was completely lost to how good it felt, and I slipped my fingers to my jeans and unbuttoned them so I could slide my hand down the front and into my panties. I wanted to be on the same cliff that he was dangling on.

"Jesus," he tipped his head back and growled the word,

letting me know that he wasn't going to be able to hang on much longer. But I didn't want this to end. I wanted to tease and torment a little longer, to push him further.

"Mmm." I pulled back for a moment, catching my breath and stroking him a couple of times, tilting my head back so I could look him in the eyes. There was something about the way he watched me when I was the one in control, something between admiration and complete devotion.

Leaning forward, I began again, swirling my tongue around the head of his cock, and a small furrow appeared above one brow as he was caught between enjoying what I was doing and enjoying the show that I was giving him by fingering myself.

"Fuck." He thrust a couple of times, as though he was practicing for how he would move when he was inside me. My body reacted to the thought of it, and I closed my eyes and opened my mouth a little more, taking him even deeper down my throat.

Suddenly, he reached down and tucked his hands beneath my arms and pulled me to my feet. He pushed me back against the door, his tongue in my mouth as he raked his fingers through my hair. My heart zinged at his touch, at the feel of him pressed against my hip.

"I need to be inside you," he murmured in my ear before turning me around so that I was facing away from him. My hands were braced against the door, and I arched my back, shooting a look over my shoulder and fluttering my lashes playfully.

"Then fuck me," I shot back, a challenge as much as an invitation. He pulled a condom from his pocket and swiftly sheathed himself, kicking off his pants and pushing mine the rest of the way down, taking my panties with them. He ran his hand over my ass appreciatively, letting out a little groan as I posed there for him. When he slid his hand around and then between my legs, I let him, needing this as much as he did. His fingers found my clit as he guided his cock toward me.

"London," he breathed in my ear as he moved into me, our bodies joining.

"Oh..." I groaned as he began to thrust, stroking my clit at the same pace and sending me into this rolling, roiling desire that felt as though it had wiped everything else from my brain.

He went slow at first, letting me get used to the feel of him, and I pushed, rocking my body back to meet his. But he soon began to pick up his pace, moving harder and deeper until he was fucking me in long, slow strokes that sent shockwaves over my entire body. He was so close to me I could feel his breath on the back of my neck as he moved inside me, the way it seemed to become more feverish and ragged as he went hard against me. The intensity of tonight satisfying me in a way I never knew that I needed. It wasn't long before I felt the orgasm building, the sensations blurring together and focusing on one goal. My mouth dropped open, and he slipped his hand around my head, tilting my face back toward him so that he could kiss me. His lips against mine were frantic, needy, his teeth catching on my lip as he let out a little groan with each thrust.

The pleasure crested and burst, my knees shaking as he looped the hand that had been between my legs around my waist to keep me upright. He thrust a few more times before finding his climax, a noise escaping him the likes of which I had never heard before. He held himself still as we both came back to reality, and I linked my fingers with his as he planted kisses over my cheek and my neck and held me so close I wasn't sure he would ever let go.

"I love you." His words were soft, and for a moment, it was as though he was reading my mind. I turned my head to kiss him, and he held himself inside me, savoring the moment.

I couldn't believe that Braden Fucking McManus was in love with me.

"I love you, London," he said again as he looked down on me.

The tears slipped from my eyes, and I could see the love on his face.

After he slid out of me, seemingly reluctantly, he went to dispose of the condom. I leaned up against the door and caught my breath, eyes still closed and not wanting to give up the moment quite yet.

"Couldn't even make it to the bed, huh?" he teased when he came back and scooped me up easily into his arms and carried me over to the bed. I felt so delicate and light in his grasp, safe against his chest. I nestled my face into his neck and let out a satisfied sigh.

He pulled a blanket over us and then rolled me over and tucked me up against his chest, wrapping his arms tight around me.

"What are you thinking about?" he asked as he leaned forward to kiss me.

"Just thinking how happy I am." I kept my eyes closed for a moment. I could feel his erection stirring against me. "Someone is ready for round two," I said playfully, I could feel his lips spread into a grin as he peppered me with soft kisses along the side of my face.

"You can't expect me not to," he murmured in my ear. "You're wiggling your ass against me."

He moved his hands over my legs and my waist and

began to grind against me gently. I wiggled my butt some more.

"You men only want one thing," I scolded him jokingly and turned my head to kiss him properly. Before I knew it, his hand was between my legs again, his fingers slipping inside me. I groaned and tipped my head back, and he ran a line of kisses up the side of my neck, his breath warming my skin as he went. He fucked me slowly with his fingers, languidly, lazily, and I found myself lost to the pleasure once more.

"I really want to fuck you right now."

"Have you got a condom?" I couldn't think straight, not with the way he was playing with me, but my brain was able to form that thought enough for me to get it out.

"Insatiable, aren't you?" he teased, as he rolled from the bed and went to grab a condom. When he returned, he was already sheathed and slid in behind me and his mouth found my neck again. When he lifted my leg a little and then slid himself into me, I was lost to the sensation of it. He had taken me from behind against the door, but this was way more intimate and intense. He looped his arm around my leg to hold me up and held me tight as he began to move.

"Holy hell." I sighed, loving the way he felt. I loved him.

"I love you." The words were still a novelty, and I couldn't help but smile. I started to move back against him, rolling my hips to take him in deeper, and soon, we had lost ourselves to the pleasure all over again. "I love you, Braden."

Braden traced one finger along the curve of my waist down over my hip to my thigh and then back up. "When did you realize you loved me?"

"That night I freaked out on you and told you to never come back. When you left, I felt a hole in my chest, and I thought I would die. I wanted to call you and tell you how sorry I was, but I felt so embarrassed by what I had said to you. I thought you would never forgive me for my words. I thought I had ruined the one thing that I had always wanted, you."

He smiled. "You couldn't have lost me that easily."

"I didn't know that though."

"Oh, London, when I saw you in the bar that first night, it did something. I can't explain it."

"It did?" I knew my question sounded childish, but his words made me feel like a teenager all over again.

"Yeah, it did."

I smiled up at him. "Don't let me go."

"Umm, never."

I laughed and ran my fingers down to his body and as he started to get hard again.

"Hmm...I think we should see if it is as good the third time."

He laughed and rolled over on top of me.

"I think I'm going to enjoy finding that one out." He kissed me and laughed.

"Me too," I said as I ran my hand down his chest.

Turned out that the third time was a charm, and after we were both spent. I yawned, stretched, and curled against his naked body, drifting to sleep in perfect contentment.

EPILOGUE

O ne Year Later...
        Braden

"I THINK that's the last box, you ready?" I turned to face my new bride.

There was a glow about her, it was happiness, and she radiated with it. I took the box from her and put it in the truck. "Come on, I made dinner for us to celebrate."

"But we've been inside a million times."

"I know but tonight will be our first night in the new house, plus I got Holland and Paris to promise that they wouldn't come over."

London giggled. "How long do you think that'll last?"

"Not long. That's why we have to enjoy it now. I mean, come on, we're only next door."

Once London had agreed to marry me, the first thing we needed to decide was where to live. I loved her sisters, but I didn't want to live with them the entire time. So after a long discussion, it was decided that we'd build a house closer to the barn that handled all of the ranch workings since that was London's true love. It made the three sisters think about how they were going to work the business going forward. Paris had no interest in leaving the main house, and that was where the garden was, so it worked for her. Holland loved the stables, but there was no place to build a house since the property next to it belonged to Reid. So Paris and Holland were going to be together in the main house until they could figure something out.

"What did you make?"

"It's a surprise."

"Dinner? Since when is dinner a surprise?"

"Since I decided to make it so." I smiled at her as she stuck her tongue out and pouted. I closed the door and then walked around to get into my side of the truck.

"Umm, look at the house." I pointed over to the front porch where Paris and Holland were waving and making crude gestures. Having been raised an only child it had taken an entire year to get used to having sisters.

"See you later," London hollered at her sisters.

Does he know yet? Paris mouthed and did a weird set of mime gestures.

"Do I know what?" London didn't look at me. "Honey, do I know what?"

"Oh stop, you aren't the only one with surprises."

London held up her middle finger to Paris as we drove off, all of the equivalent of one street block to the house we'd built, our house, the one London and I had designed and picked everything out for, took my breath away.

"Stay there." I jumped out and raced around, opening her door and then scooping her into my arms. I carried her up the few steps and over the threshold. "Welcome to your new home, Mrs. McManus." I kissed my wife, who'd only been my wife for one month.

"Why thank you, dear husband." She gave me a quick kiss. "I'm starving." As to drive home the point her stomach growled.

I carried her into the house and straight through to the dinning room before setting her on her feet. Everything about this felt right, this was home, not just in the structure itself but London, she was my home. Once she sat and I pushed her chair back in, I made my way to the kitchen.

Walking to the stove, I began fixing two plates of spaghetti. Just like I'd done on our very first date at my house, only it was our very first night in our house.

"Here you are, my lady." I set the plate in front of her, and before I had even made it to my side of the table and sat she'd taken a bite.

"Hmm, yummy, so delicious!"

"I'm glad you like it."

"I don't think you've ever cooked one thing that I didn't like."

"Maybe you're just easy to please," I said.

"I don't know, maybe you should take me into the bedroom and please me that way too," she said, a lascivious look in her eyes before she took another bite.

"Woman, you are insatiable."

"But trying to satiate me is half the fun, right?"

"You are far too good for my ego."

"You know what?" London put down her fork and stared at me intently.

"No, what?" I smiled back.

"I think that when we have children that we should name them after the places we love."

"I don't think a kid is going to want the name London's pussy for the rest of their life."

"I'm serious."

"So am I, you said places that I love."

"I'm being serious." Tears filled her eyes.

"I'm sorry, honey, I was just teasing. What kind of places were you thinking?" I had no clue why London was getting so upset over a hypothetical question.

"My mom named me and my sisters and I after places she wanted to see. I was thinking that if we had a girl, we could name her Tera. You know, it means Earth, and we both have, or rather I had, Irish last names. Wouldn't Tera Kelly McManus, be a nice name?"

Her words slowly sank in. "London, are you trying to tell me something?"

She nodded slowly and smiled.

I pulled her into my arms and spun her around. I couldn't believe I was going to be a dad.

"You're making me dizzy. Put me down."

"I'm sorry. I'm sorry." I set her down then yanked up her shirt, dropped to my knees, and placed fervent kisses on her belly. "I'm sorry, baby. Daddy is so happy."

"Jesus." She pressed her hands onto my shoulders and pushed me away so she could slide back into her seat.

"What? I'm just talking to my daughter."

"Daughter, how do you know it's a daughter?"

"We aren't naming a son Tera, and well, your family seems to be strong with girls so I think that we're safe."

"You do realize that I don't have anything to do with the gender, right?"

"Of course I knew that."

"But if the baby is a boy, we could always name him

Terance." London twirled some pasta onto her fork and shoved it into her mouth.

"No. That's a horrid name. He'd get beaten up for a name like that. How about that woman, the dark haired one from the Tera movie."

"You mean Gone With the Wind?"

I nodded as I took a bite.

"No, we are not naming a daughter Scarlet. Scarlet was a bitch, and she'd end up being called Scarlet the harlot or something or another. We can't use your dad's name either, too many kids know the nickname for Richard."

"Maybe we should make a list of names that we don't want."

"Oh that's stupid, there can't be that many." London stood up and began clearing the plates while I started putting away the leftovers. "No to Lucy because some boy will start Lucy Goosey and pinching her ass. No to Charlotte for the same reason as Scarlet."

"I've got an idea." I took the plates from her hand and set them on the counter.

"What?" London gave me a doubtful look.

"I think better when I'm in the shower. I believe that if we shower together, the perfect name might come to us. If not, we'll just have to shower together every day until he or she gets here."

"Umm, I like the way you think, Mr. McManus. Lead the way."

Stetson Playlist- London & Braden

Shoot Me Straight- Brothers Osborne
I Hate Love Songs- Kelsea Ballerini
Lose My Mind- Brett Eldredge
Fancy- Reba McEntire
Gonna Wanna Tonight- Chase Rice
Kiss You In The Morning- Michael Ray
I Do- Morgan Evans
Inside Your Heaven- Carrie Underwood

THANK YOU

- Editing by AW Editing
- Proofreading by Karen Boston
- Proofreading Emily Kirkpatrick
- Cover Design by F Squared
- Publicity and Marketing - L.Woods PR
- Bitch extraordinaire- Tina Snider

🌹 OMG- can you believe it, my fifth novel. Thank you to all of you for supporting me on this journey. Thank you to the gang!!! I love the Iron Orchids although we seldom stay on topic, we are a hoot.

🌹 Ashley, life has been chaotic. Need I say more? You are the world's greatest editor. I only hope that I am half as great as a client.

🌹 Veronica, thank you for putting up with my CDO, as we both know it is not OCD since that is not in proper alphabetical order.

💋 Peggy, thank you for enduring the heartless author that decided to slaughter a horse in a book.

MEET DANIELLE

Before becoming a romance writer, Danielle was a body double for Heidi Klum and a backup singer for Adele. Now, she spends her days trying to play keep away from Theo James, who won't stop calling her or asking her out.

And all of this happens before she wakes up and faces reality where in fact she is a 50-something mom with grown kids. She's been married longer than Theo's been alive, and she now gets her kicks riding a Harley.

As far as her body, she can thank Ben & Jerry's for that, as well as gravity and vodka. But she says that she could never be Adele's backup since she never stops saying the F-word long enough to actually sing.

Danielle writes about kickass women with even better shoes and the men that try to tame them (silly, silly men).

LETS SOCIALIZE

💜 Website: www.daniellenorman.com
💜 Twitter: @1daniellenorman
💜 Facebook fan page: @authordaniellenorman
💜 Instagram: @1daniellenorman
💜 Amazon Author Page @daniellenorman
💜 Goodreads @daniellenorman
💜 Bookbub: @daniellenorman
💜 Book + Main: @daniellenorman
💜 Official Iron Orchids Fan Group : on facebook
💜 Newsletter: http://bit.ly/DNnews

ALSO BY DANIELLE NORMAN

<u>**Available in Ebook, Paperback, and Audio.**</u>

Nothing says friendship like a group of women who can laugh together, stand up for another, be uniquely different, and still have one thing in common...they all ride motorcycles.

We've got ourselves a gang, not like a we're badass gang, but more like a *we make this shit look good kind of gang.*

SNEAK PEEK- ENOUGH, IRON ORCHIDS

Ariel

Moving to the happiest fucking place on Earth had nothing to do with fairy tales or finding my Prince Charming. Thanks to my daddy, I no longer believed in magic or happily ever afters. I landed in this city because this was the land of hotels, conventions, and destination weddings, which meant it was my best bet at becoming an event planner.

I didn't hate being a seamstress, but it wasn't my dream, it was my mama's. I never told her that I'd rather be on the other side, planning the events where people wore the fancy clothes, costumes, and uniforms.

I never got the chance.

During my freshman year of high school, she had her first stroke, spoke with a slur, and relied a little more on me. But just before my senior year, Mama had her second stroke, and someone needed to keep the business going to pay the bills, so I took over. Because Daddy was long gone, he had no use for an invalid wife, and no interest in raising a teenage daughter who hated him. I told myself repeatedly that Mama would have wanted me to follow my dream, even if it meant hers was gone. Though, I doubted that included buying a motorcycle.

I BRUSHED the wetness away then strapped on my helmet and headed to my motorcycle. Ever since binge watching Sons of Anarchy, I wanted to be badass. Okay, not like crime badass. Just the I-look-cool-onthis-bike kind of badass. So, after I unpacked my last box, I went out and purchased a Harley Sportster. I couldn't wait to start the engine and let the wind whip across my face. It was cathartic. As the engine roared to life, I replayed the words my teacher said just a few weeks ago during motorcycle safety class.

Ease up on the throttle.

Hold steady.

Don't freak.

The bike will go where your eyes go.

I found myself twisting the throttle a little more than I should have, and a small smile pulled at my lips. I shifted gears and headed to the service road around the Mall at Millennia, Orlando's version of Rodeo Drive. Since I lived in metro Orlando, finding somewhere to practice riding wasn't easy. There were always constant road improvements or tourists who drove like idiots reversing down the interstate because they missed the fucking exit. So, the rarely traversed area behind the mall was one of the best places to practice. It was also one of the only places I'd practiced. I stayed within a five-mile radius of my home, but I needed to get comfortable and feel confident so I could take my bike out for a long ride, let the sun shine down on my face and forget the reality that was my life.

After a few laps around the mall, I pulled my bike into a

parking spot, headed inside to grab a drink, and was walking back out to my bike when two men dressed all in black cut between two cars. They reminded me of Crabbe and Goyle from the Harry Potter movies, and I was still watching them from the corner of my eye when they broke into a run. There was nothing oaf-like or klutzy about them. Maybe they had just robbed Tiffany's or Cartier? That didn't seem right, though. There were no security guards chasing them. No alarms going off or police cruisers peeling into the lot. Eyebrows dipping, I paused. Watching.bThe two men zigzagged through another section of cars, and the one on the left pointed in my direction. In that earth-shattering moment it connected—they were after me. I ran. Fuck. I had no clue what to do. I would never be able to start my bike and get away quick enough. Their footsteps got closer then stopped. I turned around just as the two men separated, one going left the other going right, moving in an arc around me. They were corralling me like a caged animal.

"Help!" I shouted just before a hand clamped over my mouth.

"Shut the fuck up, bitch," a husky voice commanded.

I didn't. I continued to try to scream as I kicked and hit him. Biting. I raked my nails down his forearm, his face, his shoulder—wherever I could dig my nails. I wasn't going with these men willingly.

People say your life flashes before your eyes in times of crisis, when what they mean is that you replay your life in slow motion. In those brief moments, it seemed as if I relived that day when everything seemed to unravel. Mama sitting at her sewing table as she looked up and hollered, "Close that door. You weren't born in a barn." And I'd had it, she kept forgiving him.

"Why do you stay married to him? All day long Billie

Sue Werner ran around school telling the entire freshman class that her mama saw Daddy parked by the railroad tracks with Ms. Kinney, and they were 'going at it.' It's the same thing Daddy does almost every night just with different women. You know it, I know it, the whole town knows it, Mama. And they're laughing at us." I marched back through the house and slammed the door shut. This was just one of the many things I hated about living in a small town, everybody knew your business, and nothing ever changed.

"You go get your homework done, you hear me?"

"Yes, I hear you. But do you hear me? Mama, I'm serious. I'm leaving.

I can take no more."

That was when Mama's face took on an ashen appearance and she collapsed. I learned real fast how wrong I was, I could take more. In fact, it was shoved down my throat, heaped on my shoulders, and I was still taking it.

The brief flash from my past was shattered by the smell of days old sweat on the man holding me. My body revolted, my mouth went watery, and my stomach lurched with the sour taste curdling on my tongue. I was going to vomit, and there was nothing I could do to stop it.

"Fucking watch it, man. We ain't supposed to hurt her, just scare her." The guy I nicknamed Crabbe had a Hispanic accent and seemed a bit uncomfortable about what they were doing. I broke free from the Goyle-dude as he argued back.

Scare me? Scare me? What the fuck? "Help!" My shout rang out across the parking lot. "Fine. You scared me. Let me go!"

They came at me again, obviously not convinced that I was scared enough. They circled me, Crabbe in front and

Goyle-dude at my back. The guy behind me wrapped his arms around my chest, restraining me and lifted me off the ground. The toes of my left shoe scraped the concrete, giving me just enough leverage to pull my leg back and aim
   for the fat guy's nuts.

"Help!" I shouted again and again until my throat burned. Someone had to hear me. There had to be someone! I refused to cry, not yet, not there, I needed to get a grip on at least one of these men. Anything. Anywhere. These bastards, whoever they were, were not going to get away with what they were trying to do. I had to break free long enough to pull off their damn masks, at least one of their masks. If I survived, I wanted to be able to identify these sons of bitches. I didn't get the chance, though. Untrimmed nails bit into my ankles as the other thug grabbed my legs.

"Let's go," Goyle-dude ordered.

I bucked, twisted, and tried to get away as they carried me like a piece of furniture.

Then I heard it, a shout in the distance. "Police! Freeze!"

In their haste to escape, the men dropped me, I scrambled to right myself and get my feet under me. My head snapped back, pain shot through my scalp as one of the men grabbed a fistful of my hair and slammed me forward. My face met the hood of a car with a sickening crack. The wet heat of my own blood and searing pain were the only things I registered before the man yanked back one more time. I didn't have time to put my hands up as my face barreled toward a window and I hit the car again, this time with enough force to knock me out. I awoke on the ground, the burning hot pavement seared through my skin and deep down to my bones. Tiny pieces of gravel and sand pressed into my skin. I wasn't sure how long I'd been lying there, but

I was hyperaware and could feel every single pebble and grain. Gentle fingers wrapped around my wrist that rested at my side. I felt the brush of a watchband against my palm and scratch of calluses over my skin. Somehow, I was alert enough to process that this was a man's hand. He pressed two fingers to the underside of my wrist. It took a few more seconds to realize that he was checking for a pulse, and then the fear set in that my attackers were back. I tried to get up, but I couldn't move, I ached too badly.

"Help," I begged, but my voice sounded like a gurgle, a sound that even I didn't recognize escaping my lips.

Lights flashed around me. I didn't understand where all the lights were coming from. My mind too clouded with fear, it took me several seconds to realize that they were prisms dancing in tiny shards of glass that surrounded me. The hand on my wrist was gone, and a moment later, a man's face came into my field of vision.

"Can you hear me? I am Deputy Kayson Christakos; I'm here to rescue you. Paramedics are on the way. Don't try to move. You're safe."

Blink.

Our eyes locked.

Blink.

I saw stars. No . . . a star. Then I passed out, again.

48792135R00117

Made in the USA
Columbia, SC
12 January 2019